P9-EJZ-842

IN CAMERA

and other stories

Also by
ROBERT WESTALL

IN CAMERA

and other stories

ROBERT WESTALL

Scholastic Inc.
New York

Library of Congress Cataloging-in-Publication Data

Westall, Robert.
In camera and other stories / Robert Westall.
p. cm.
Summary: Five tales of psychological suspense and the supernatural.

ISBN 0-590-45920-1

1. Horror tales, England. [1. Horror stories. 2. Supernatural-Fiction. 3. Short stories.]
I. Title.
PZ7.W51953Tr 1993
[Fic]—dc20 92-13815
CIP
AC

12 11 10 9 8 7 6 5 4 3 2 1 3 4 5 6 7 8/9

Printed in the U.S.A. 37

First Scholastic printing, February 1993

For Lindy
who registered, amongst other things,
an idea.

Contents

In Camera

I first met Phil Marsden when he reported a burglary. The Super sent me. Only routine we thought, but the people who live on Birkbeck Common are rich and can turn nasty if not handled diplomatically.

I rang his chimes and saw him swimming towards me through the pebble glass of his front door. My first thought was that he was quite little.

His first thought . . . he looked crushed as people do when they've just been burgled. Then his little face lit up and he said:

'Helloooooh!'

As if I was the Easter Bunny and a Christmas hamper all rolled into one. I have that effect on men; it makes life as a policewoman very difficult. I showed him my warrant card to take the smile off his face. He read it with great care, then made the remark I'd learned to dread.

'It's a fair cop!'

I suppose it was funny the first time somebody said it.

'If we can get on, sir?' I said it as severely as I could. I work hard at being severe; even scraping back my hair into the severest bun possible, so tight I give myself a headache. But that only draws attention to my ears, which I have been told are shell-like more often than I care to remember . . .

I sat down briskly with my notebook out. He sat with that stupid look on his face, admiring my legs. But I eventually got out of him that there was no sign of a break-in and that he had a very expensive burglar alarm, which he was sure he'd left switched on that morning, as he never forgot things like that.

'They must've nobbled it.'

'That type are very hard to nobble. Have you checked to see if it's still working?'

It was working perfectly; *that* took the look off his face.

'Not nobbled,' I said. 'Just switched off. By somebody who knew the code. And by the look of your front door, they had a key, too.'

'Impossible. I've only got three keys. One with my neighbour and two on my key-ring.'

I established that the helpful neighbour was a famous barrister who had no need to resort to part-time burglary to keep the wolf from the door. Then he fetched his key-ring and found one of his keys missing.

'It's somebody you know,' I said. He spent the next half hour telling me his friends weren't *like* that. Meanwhile, I found out what was missing. Usual dreary round, hi-fi, video, TV, gold cufflinks. But the thing he was most upset about was three antique cameras, God help us. I didn't know people collected antique cameras; I thought they just threw them away when they stopped working.

'Show me.'

He led me to a room quite unlike the others. No designer furniture, just plain shelves filled with old cameras. Things in mahogany and brass, big as briefcases. Tatty little Bakelite Kodaks from the fifties, pre-war things with bellows, Brownie boxes.

The room was also a darkroom, with big black-and-white prints hung up to dry. Off-beat views of the world, taken from funny angles. That was what first intrigued me about him.

'Which cameras have gone?'

He showed me three sad gaps. 'Two Leica IIcs and a very old Hasselblad. The only ones worth anything.'

That made me prick my shell-like ears. Few burglars are experts on antique cameras.

'Do you show your friends this lot?'

He looked pained. 'They're not the sort to be interested.'

I betted not; this place was where his funny little heart and soul were; very few of his lovely friends would be shown this.

'But you showed *somebody*? Recently?'

'Only Rodney. Rodney Smith. But he wouldn't . . . I was at school with him.'

'Were you and Mr Smith *alone*?'

'There was his girl-friend. Big dishy brunette. Madeleine Something. But she wasn't interested. She was half-pissed. Kept stroking his back and giggling. Wanted bed. Not that Rodney would be my cup of tea . . . '

Well, it transpired that they'd all gone out to the pub before dinner. And Rodney and Madeleine had watched while he banged in the code on the burglar alarm. And Phil had left his keys in the pocket of his raincoat, hanging up in the pub . . .

'But,' he kept on saying stupidly, 'but . . . '

To cut a long story short, his mate Rodney didn't have any criminal record, beyond drunk-driving. But Madeleine Something had a record as long as your arm, as well as a little friend we knew very well called Spike Malone. And the Met were just about to raid Spike's Mum's tower block flat . . .

Two days later, I laid the cameras at Phil's feet. At least metaphorically, for they were still required as evidence.

'Hey, you're bright, Sergeant,' he said. 'Sherlock Holmes rides again, eh?'

I could've hit him, except I was on duty. But he got his act together in time and asked me out to dinner. Which I accepted as I like good food but a sergeant's pay doesn't run to it. And we sort of went on from there. Though I never took him seriously, because he was an inch shorter than me. But he was fun. An innocent really. And I had a maternal urge to tidy up his little life for him.

At the first of his parties that I went to, somebody lit up a reefer. I got my coat and left before you could say 'New Scotland Yard' and we had the mother and father of a row over the phone afterwards. He promised to get rid of certain people from his life, and he must've done, because I never spotted anything dicey again.

The most interesting friends he had left were John Malpas the painter and his wife Melanie. John wasn't your typical artist. Looked like a worried banker and worked at his paintings like a stevedore, all the hours God sent. He was always so busy talking at table that you had to throw out his glass of wine afterwards. Melanie was painfully thin but very elegant with the most enormous grey eyes. I approved of the fact that unlike most of Phil's friends, they were actually married. Terminally married. They really needed each other, like my Mum and Dad do. So I felt comfortable with them.

That Saturday morning, Phil and I'd been up the Portobello Market and Phil had acquired yet another camera. A 1930s Zeiss Ikon. He had three Zeiss Ikons already, but you know what collectors are. But what had really turned him on was that this Zeiss had a roll of exposed film still inside it. A random slice of somebody else's life, Phil called it, and vanished into his precious darkroom to develop it, leaving me to finish getting dinner ready, because John and Melanie were coming. Ambitious cook, Phil. Always does the main dishes, soaking them overnight in wine or oil, till you can't tell whether you're eating beef or lamb. But he's not keen on doing all the fiddly bits.

He was in the darkroom so long, I had to lay the table as well. And give John and Melanie their first drink and dips. When he finally emerged for dinner, after much screaming and hammering on the darkroom door, he was still in his oldest jeans and a tee-shirt that stank of developer. He was as high as a kite; you would almost have thought he was on a trip. He held a handful of big ten-by-eight enlargements that dripped fixer on the carpet he'd paid thirty-five pounds a yard for.

He shoved one print at John, saying, 'What do you make of that?' and then sat with the other prints in his lap, where they made a spreading damp patch on his jeans.

Now John had one little vanity: his powers of

observation. He could never see a picture postcard, or a photo on a calendar, or even a half-finished jigsaw, without sitting down to work out what the picture was of, what time of day it had been taken and even what month of the year it was. Shouting, 'Don't you *dare* give me a clue!' I think he saw me as a rival. He was always saying that artists had greater powers of observation than any detective.

Determined not to be left out, I took my drink and went to sit beside him. The photograph, needle-sharp, was of a village green, with the parish church in the background.

That would tell him where east lay . . .

'Taken in the evening,' he said. 'Look at the length of those shadows.'

'October,' I said. 'Leaves still on the trees, but quite a lot fallen.'

'Taken after 1937,' he said. 'There's the last sort of pre-War Austin Seven.'

'But before the War,' I said, cock-a-hoop. 'There's one of those Wall's ice-cream tricycles – you know, "Stop Me and Buy One". They never came back, after the War.'

'Sergeant, I take my hat off to you!' Then he shot in, 'Pantile roofs – that means somewhere near the east coast.'

'There's a flint wall – the southern part of the east coast. East Anglia . . . '

'Look at the size of the church. That's Suffolk or I'm a Dutchman.'

'There's a white weatherboarded house – you don't get many of those north of Woodbridge.' Then I played my trump-card. 'A Sunday evening – kids in their

Sunday best, people coming out of church, women carrying prayer-books . . . '

'Damn you, Sergeant. This country's turning into a police state.' But his eyes were still scanning the photo, looking for the last word.

Phil laughed diabolically, pleased to have set us off against each other. He handed us another photograph.

'Try this, my children!'

It was the photograph of a woman, or perhaps only a girl; holding on to the door of the Austin Seven, looking shyly up into the camera.

'She's not married,' I said. 'No ring.'

'A prim miss – no nail-varnish. Ankle socks.'

'But . . . in love, I think. Very much in love. With the man who took the picture.'

'You sentimental old sergeant. I didn't know the Met had it in them.'

I was silent. Weighing up the girl. She had a shy, self-effacing way of standing. And yet her eyes were huge and glowing, and her lips parted . . . a shy girl made bold by love, I thought. And no engagement ring either. I didn't like to see such vulnerability. Then I told myself not to be an imaginative fool . . . you could read too much into faces.

'Want to know what her fellow looked like?' asked Phil. He passed another photograph. This one was much less professional, with the camera held crookedly, and the man's head hard up against the top edge. He too was leaning against the Austin Seven. It was the kind of photo an inexperienced girl might have taken . . .

'He looks very pleased with himself,' said John,

rather crossly. Was he a little in love with the girl in the photo? Was he jealous of the man? 'And old enough to be her father.'

I wasn't so sure about that. The man's hair was cut short at the back and sides, as all men's was in those days. It made his ears stick out and look huge. It also made him look middle-aged, but then that hairstyle in old photographs could make schoolboys look middle-aged.

'Eyes too close together,' said John. 'I never trust a man whose eyes are too close together.' Then he added, 'A bit of a puritan, I would say. Look at that mouth, a real thin rat-trap.'

Phil gave another of his mock sinister laughs. 'Not so sure of that. Look at this one.'

It was the girl again. Lying down in what seemed to be a woodland glade. On a tartan rug, with a straggle of items around her: Thermos flask, picnic-basket, raincoats. Her clothing was not at all disarranged, except for the skirt which had ridden up over one knee. But her smile, the glow in her eyes, stronger now . . . every hallmark of a girl who has happily made love. A lock of her hair was falling over one eye . . .

'Yes,' said John. He wriggled a little, on the sofa next to me. I think he was embarrassed because the same thought had come into his head. A very nice man, John.

'And this,' said Phil triumphantly, handing us the last print with a flourish. 'Talk about the wreck of the *Hesperus*.'

The girl still lay in the forest glade, but she lay full length now, her head resting flat against the ground, her eyes nearly shut, the mouth drooping open in a most unpleasing way . . .

I froze. I had seen such photographs too often to be mistaken. The grace of the long limbs was gone; they were as untidy as a pile of dropped garbage.

'She's dead,' I said. 'I've seen too many like her. I *know*.'

'God, I feel sick,' said John. And the next second he was running for the bathroom.

We sat round in a huddled, excited heap.

'Can't *you* do something?' Phil asked me plaintively for the fifth time.

'Not if I value my job,' I said, backing off vigorously. 'We don't know when that picture was taken or where, or who they were. We only know it was well over fifty years ago. And that last photograph is *not* evidence. It could be a trick of the light, a trick of the camera. Maybe she was just in pain, or feeling sick. We have no evidence it was even taken in England.'

'The other photo was – you said it was Suffolk.'

'That was the other photograph. They might have taken the camera overseas . . . '

'It looks like an English glade.'

'Don't you think they have glades like that in France or Germany? What the hell do you mean, an *English* glade? Are you an expert on English glades or something?' I was starting to get mad.

Poor Phil wilted and looked moodily at his expensive carpet. 'We could try and find the place,' he said feebly. 'That wouldn't do any harm. We could drive over there and make enquiries . . . '

'Have you ever tried making enquiries?' I asked savagely, remembering how many doors I'd knocked on, and my aching feet. 'If that girl was alive now, she'd be in her mid-seventies. Most of the people who knew her when she looked like that will be dead long since. Do you see yourself knocking on the door of every old granny in Suffolk saying do you remember this girl?'

'All the same,' said John thoughtfully, 'I think we ought to try. That girl's face will haunt me. I feel I owe it to her.'

I glanced at Melanie, expecting the support of some common sense from the distaff side. But her face, very sad, was watching John's. Again, I felt how close the two of them were.

At last she said, 'I think we must. It's so awful to think of him killing her, then photographing her when she was dead . . . as if he wanted to gloat over it. I don't think a man like that should be wandering about loose, however old he is, even if he's eighty. It's like those Nazi war criminals . . . it's never too late to bring them to justice.'

'Let's go over and look next weekend,' said Phil, a little smile of excitement lighting up his face, so I could have *kicked* him, for his heartlessness.

'A sort of murder holiday weekend,' I said bitterly. 'Like they lay on at hotels now. Only with an extra luxury, a real corpse.'

'C'mon,' he said. 'I know a super pub we could stay at, at Felsbrough. The cooking is out of this world . . . '

I didn't go for the food. I went to keep him out of trouble.

I didn't see him again until the next weekend, when I'd booked myself three days' leave; I had plenty of rest-days in hand.

He seemed to have regained his high spirits by the time he rang my bell. Regained them indeed, considering he was wearing a ridiculous outfit of white flannels and a pink blazer with white stripes.

'What's this – a fancy-dress ball?' His little face fell, and I felt a bit of a brute.

'Just getting in the spirit of the thing – Albert Campion and all that . . . 1930s.'

'I suppose I should give you a clip over the Lugg . . . '

Worse was to follow when I locked my flat and went downstairs. Parked next to my Metro was a huge green object with brass headlights and no roof.

'What's that supposed to be?'

'Bentley four-litre. 1936. Borrowed it off a mate – he owed me a favour.'

From the back seat of the monstrosity, John and Melanie waved. They were wearing matching and tasteful tweed suits and deerstalker hats. Melanie's outfit even had a cape. They looked exceedingly chic, and I felt I was joining a circus.

'Where do I put my luggage?' I said tightly. 'Where's the boot?'

'Hasn't got much of a boot,' said Phil. 'I'll strap it on the back with the rest.'

God, all that great length, which would be hell to park, and no boot. Even the spare wheel was strapped on the outside. That was the trouble with that monster. It was all outside and no inside. Most of the inside appeared to be occupied by the engine. The accommodation for passengers would've disgraced a First World War fighter plane.

'I hope it doesn't rain.'

'There is a hood. But it takes about twenty minutes to put up. My mate *has* done it occasionally. But the weather forecast's good.'

Needless to say, they'd found room for a food hamper between John and Melanie. There was the expected clink of champagne bottles, as they shifted uncomfortably in their leather seats.

'Hold on to your hats! We're off!'

I must say Phil seemed to know how to handle it; he was always good at mechanical things. I never actually felt in danger of my life, though the flashy way he showed off his skill at double de-clutching was a little grating after a while. And I suppose there is something in that old saying about the joy of feeling the wind in your hair; fortunately I keep mine in a tight bun, as I said. But what with digging flies out of my eye, and having to scream every remark at the top of my voice over the vroom of the exhausts, and worrying about the straps holding my luggage on the back . . . it didn't improve my temper.

Nonetheless, it didn't stop the conversation.

'We've made a bit of progress since last week,' said Phil. 'I talked to a feller about that film in the camera. He said it was impossible for a roll of exposed undeveloped negatives to have lasted since the 1930s. Yet they *are* from the 1930s . . .'

'You call that making *progress*?' I snapped (if you can snap while screaming at the top of your voice).

Yet it spooked me, what he said. As a policewoman, I don't go for the inexplicable. I would like a world without the inexplicable. I felt a shiver run down my spine, as if somebody had walked over my grave.

And John and Melanie in the back didn't help any. John had spent the week going over the big prints with a magnifying glass. I began to realise that he had an obsessional personality, and he was obsessed.

'That bloke . . . his hand on the car door . . . he's wearing a wedding ring on the third finger of his left hand. He's got a ring, and she hasn't . . . that's a motive for him doing her in.'

'What do you mean, a motive?'

'He might have got her pregnant . . . she might have been threatening to go to his wife and spill the beans. So he had to shut her up, hadn't he?'

'We haven't even proved she's dead yet.' The whole thing began to disgust me. John and Melanie were high on what I suppose a bad novelist would call the thrill of the chase.

You don't get the police talking about the thrill of the chase. Or if you do, avoid them, because they're very bad police. If you talk about the thrill of the chase, it means you've decided who's guilty, before you can prove it. Oh, you have that temptation inside you all the time, but you sit on it and sit on it and never let it take you over . . .

'I've found something else,' said John, not at all abashed. 'There's a signpost on the village green in the first print – just in front of the church. You can't read the names on it, even with a magnifying glass. They're out of focus. But you can count the *letters* in the names, as blobs. There are five letters in the top name, and twelve in the bottom name.'

'What good is that? Lots of place names have five letters.'

'Yes, but not many have twelve, even in East Anglia, which is famous for long names. I've been over the road atlas, and I can only find four. Tattingstone, Wickhambrook and Grundisburgh in Suffolk, and Wethersfield in Essex. It gives us places to start. I suggest we eliminate Wickhambrook first – it's furthest from the sea, and the least likely to have pantiles on the roofs . . . '

'We'll take the M11,' said Phil. 'Show you what the old girl can do.' He put his foot down.

The old girl showed us what she could do. Once, before I put *my* foot down and made Phil take his off, she did well over a hundred. It was very painful. The slipstream came round the tiny windscreen and hit us in the face like a mob throwing half-bricks. And the poor old thing was straining every sprocket; I thought she was going to blow up on us. And then, of course, the modern cars, the Jags and Mercs and big BMWs, began to want to show us what they were made of . . . and since I knew they could do a hundred and thirty without more than a whisper of a whistle . . . We were attracting more male attention than a bitch on heat.

I finally got Phil to cut it to eighty, and that was bad enough. I didn't fancy being pulled up by a jam-butty car for speeding, even as a passenger. They give you such a look . . .

Once we had turned off for Wickhambrook, and I had breath to think, a nasty idea came floating into my mind out of my past. The medieval idea, from Chaucer's day, of the Ship of Fools. Wealthy fools voyaging to their own destruction.

Only we were a Car of Fools.

* * *

Of course, Wickhambrook was nothing like the photograph. They hadn't expected it to be. You don't get a signpost saying Wickhambrook in Wickhambrook. You drive round Wickhambrook in ever increasing circles, looking at church towers. A bit like a steeple-chase, because the church in our photo certainly had a spectacular steeple. What John referred to as a broach-spire . . .

It was quite fun at first. I had no idea there were so many kinds of church towers. Round ones, ones with octagonal tops, ones with four pinnacles and ones with eight, ones with spectacular gargoyles and even ones with flat plain tops. Needle-spires and broach-spires. I owe all my extensive knowledge of church towers to that weekend.

And just about the time my head began to spin, they got discouraged and had lunch in a sweet meadow in the sunshine. With the champagne, which always improves my temper.

After lunch, we drove on to Tattingstone. After they had despaired of Tattingstone, we went on and despaired of Grundisburgh.

It was when they had reached the point of total despair, when reality was at last breaking in on them, when they were talking about going on to the hotel and the whole thing might have collapsed into a harmless weekend, that I had to go and set them off again.

I don't like being beaten, you see. So I was still keeping my eyes open. And then I saw something. Nothing at all like a steeple, but it was a church just the same. Only this church didn't have a tower at all . . .

I saw a bus outside the church. A luxury touring bus, disgorging a stream of elegant and sprightly pensioners, who were hung about with cameras, binoculars and clipboards. A cultural course on Suffolk churches, in full swing. And I simply got Phil to stop the car, walked over to them, picked out the course leader, who was the only one without camera, binoculars and clipboard, and showed him our photograph.

'Bless me,' he said, pushing up his bifocals on to his impressive forehead and squinting at the photo closely. 'That's Bendham, before it lost its spire; in the great gale of 1976 . . . '

'But we've *been* to Bendham. It's nothing like. Just a tower peeping above great trees. And no village green.'

He twinkled at me. 'In the country, trees grow a lot in fifty years. And sadly, developers move in . . . '

I must say, Albert Campion and the two Sherlock Holmeses were not as pleased as I thought they'd be. Downright peevish.

But it *was* Bendham. The post office was still the same.

By then, it was time for a shower before dinner. Their stomachs took over and their brains went dead.

I bought a *Sunday Times* in the hotel next morning, and read right through it while they got on with their tomfoolery. The plan was to seek out old ladies within a ten-mile radius of Bendham.

I had pointed out that the best place to catch old ladies in the countryside on a Sunday morning was coming out of church. After that, the old ladies would sensibly go home, cook their roast lunch and have an afternoon snooze till it was time to go to church for Evensong . . .

They'd agreed with this. But next morning Phil had a hangover, and the breakfast was out of this world, and I couldn't get them moving before eleven. Perhaps it was as well. The vicars might have disapproved of a lunatic dressed as Albert Campion frightening their parishioners in their own churchyard. By the time we reached the first village, however, Matins was over and there wasn't a vicar or an old lady in sight.

What there was was a lot of small boys, born after 1975, drawn by the sight of the car, and even more middle-aged men, born after 1945, on their way to the pub. I suppose that damned car did help in a way . . .

Through them, Phil tracked down some old ladies in their rose-covered lairs, and knocked on their pretty white doors. Most of the old ladies thought he was on a promotion campaign for a new sort of washing powder, and were avid for coupons, free samples and chances to win £100,000 without committing themselves to buying anything.

But none of them knew the girl in the photograph, though some of them knew an Austin Seven from a Singer Ten.

As I said, I read the *Sunday Times* right down to the Stock Exchange news, and let Phil exhaust himself with his own deadly charm.

Again, it might have trailed off into a normal Sunday, with drinks and crisps in a pub and then a long expensive lunch.

But I had finished the *Sunday Times* and I was getting bored.

'Has it occurred to you,' I said to Phil as he leaned exhausted against the bonnet, 'that if your girl was murdered when you think, she didn't live around here very long? Whereas your murderer, if, as you think, he got away with it, may have lived round here very much longer?'

'You mean . . . show them *his* photograph?'

'Yes, my sweet love.'

He almost vaulted the last old lady's gate, he was so filled with renewed inspiration.

And then he came back, looking very solemn and important, and my heart went down into my boots.

'Got 'im,' he said. 'He was the local doctor. Dr Hargreaves. Lived in Berpesford till he retired in 1967.'

'A doctor,' said John, suddenly abandoning a lump of the *Sunday Times* he'd pinched off me. 'Doctors have more ways of killing people than ordinary folk . . . '

'Doctors,' said Melanie dreamily, 'like Dr Crippen and Dr Buck Ruxton . . .' She reeled off a list of famous murdering doctors.

God, would you credit it? Bored farce to high drama in ten seconds. The atmosphere grew positively hysterical. I thought it was a good thing we had a police force. If it was left to the general public . . .

'Have you got his old address? Might as well see where he lived . . . and there's a very good pub in this guide, only about three miles from Berpesford,' added John.

After an excellent lunch, we found the house. Phil knocked at the front door, asked after the good doctor, and came back looking very disgruntled.

'They haven't a clue where he went. They'd never even *heard* of him. They've only lived there for a year, and they bought the house off some Americans, who bought it off a civil engineer who worked in Ipswich.'

'Honestly,' said John indignantly. 'There's just no continuity in village life any more. Rich outsiders moving in, not caring about the place, not staying five minutes . . . bloody *yuppies*.'

They sat for a long time, glaring at the house, as if willing the pillared front door and Virginia creeper to give them a clue. After a while the people inside noticed us, and began glaring back.

'Let's go. Before they call the police,' I said.

They pulled up in a lay-by, and sat and talked things over. The best they could come up with was that we should backtrack to all the old ladies we had already spoken to, to ask them if they knew where the good doctor had retired to.

It was not a good idea. It's hard to remember which old lady you've spoken to, in a village where you've only been once. And we'd been to so many villages that I never wanted to see a pretty Suffolk village again, as long as I lived. We slowly foundered in a mass of argument.

'I'm sure it's that street on the left; I remember turning by the pub with the green shutters.'

'I don't think it's this village at all; the church was set back among trees and it had a smaller tower.'

'That was *Tattersham*, you idiot.'

'Fettersham, you mean!'

What old ladies we did find were grumpy at being disturbed again from their naps. They thought the good doctor had retired to Framlingham, Hedingham, Swannington, Walsingham and Clacton respectively. They all said he would be very old by now, well over eighty, and two thought they'd heard he'd died. The only thing they were agreed about was that he had been a wonderful doctor, whom they'd never forget as long as they lived.

Then it began to rain. John and Phil had a marvellous swearing-match over putting up the folding hood, which took much longer than twenty minutes. It reduced the interior of the car to a small dim rabbit-hutch, with yellowing celluloid windows.

Phil said the hood was genuine and authentic.

Melanie said it was leaking in at least three places.

It also obscured Phil's view to the rear, so that he crunched the precious love-object slightly, getting out of a narrow parking space.

He was reduced to a sweating babbling wreck, thinking what the good mate who had loaned him the car would say, and how much the repair would cost him. I gathered he might be drummed out of his city bank, as the mate was considerably senior to him . . .

In the end, they slunk back to the hotel with their tails between their legs, and I went and had a hot shower and changed. I was idly lounging around, waiting for Phil to knock on my door for pre-dinner drinks, when I noticed my room had a telephone.

And of course a local telephone directory.

And, ever so casually, to satisfy my own curiosity, I picked it up and looked up the name 'Hargreaves'.

There was only half a column of Hargreaveses; and a Dr L. Hargreaves sat halfway down it. He lived in Framlingham.

I sat paralysed.

I was a copper; and coppers become coppers because they believe strongly in law and order, and in making the punishment fit the crime; and as they tell you at training school, a copper is never off-duty.

But this man must be so old, and it was all so long ago, and the only evidence I had was one photographic negative that I'd been told couldn't possibly have survived for fifty years. And I wasn't even on my own patch. I thought of trying to explain it all to some grim, cynical, stolid local Superintendent and I thought he'd give me a pitying look and tell me to run away and play. He'd have a word with my own Super, and I'd be the divisional joke. It's hard enough to get any credence as a woman copper, and this could *destroy* me.

At that point, Phil walked in without knocking. He'd never done that before. I don't know if he was trying to catch me running about stark naked or what.

Instead, his hopeful little eye fell on the open telephone directory. And he got it in one. I mean, he's not stupid, just childish.

'You've *got* him!'

'There is a Dr Hargreaves in the book,' I said coldly.

We had another terrific conference over the crisps and drinks. That awful hunting look had come back into their eyes and I hated them. Talk about blood lust . . . their only problem was whether they should corner their fiend in human form before or after dinner.

I used all the arguments I could: that he was so old, that he might be the son, that he might be a different Dr Hargreaves altogether. It was no use. They were set on their bit of fun.

'There'd be no harm in ringing him up,' said Phil. 'Find out if it *is* him.'

'No,' I said.

'Well if you won't, I will.'

That I couldn't allow. He'd go in like a bull in a china shop; he might give the old boy a fatal heart attack.

So I went back up to my room and rang the good doctor's number. They all clustered round to listen.

I knew it was him, the moment he answered. The voice was clear, but faint and a little wavering. His breathing was much louder than his talking. I knew he was not only old, but sick.

'You won't know me, Dr Hargreaves,' I said, 'but I've just come across a camera that I think used to belong to you. And there was a roll of film in it. I thought you might like to see the prints we got from it . . . '

After all, what else could I say?

I heard his sharp intake of breath. I was expecting him to put the phone down on me, or at least begin to bluster. But he only said, almost normally:

'The Zeiss Ikon? I've been waiting for you a long, long time, my dear. I began to doubt that you'd ever come.'

His voice was calm, resigned. As if he truly had been waiting for me. He was so calm and sure, I grew a little afraid. Then he said:

'Would you like to bring the photographs over? This evening?'

Because I was afraid, because I knew he *was* the one, I said, 'I have three friends with me.'

'Bring them. They will be quite welcome. Nine o'clock?'

I looked at the avid faces crowding round me, listening to both sides of the conversation. All I could do was say yes.

He gave me directions on how to get there, and rang off.

His garden was an old person's garden, small but as neat as a pin. The knocker was brass, a fox's face, and highly polished. There was a general air of quiet prosperity, and the smell of old age as he opened the door.

It was the man in the photograph all right. Wrinkles gather and gather, but bones don't change. His eyes were still too close together, and his mouth even more like a rat-trap. He had been tall, but now he stooped over two sticks. His hands clenched on the sticks like an old tree's roots clench into the soil.

'Come in, come in.' He looked at my friends one by one. Not one of them had the guts to look him in the face. I thought of juries, who will not look at the prisoner in the dock when they have found him guilty.

He asked us to sit down; offered us a drink, which we all declined. I could not tell if his hands were trembling from fear, or whether they always trembled like that.

When he had slowly settled himself and laid one stick carefully on each side of his chair, I gave him the first photograph.

He smiled, remotely. 'Bendham. It's changed so

much, I wonder you were able to find it. And my old Austin Seven. I had it until 1950. Then I was able to afford something better . . . '

Then I handed him the photo of himself. And he smiled remotely again and said:

'That's still how I imagine myself, in my mind's eye. These days the mirror is always rather a shock. You just can't believe you're getting old, and the older you get, the less you believe it. But there I stand, on the verge of middle age. Still hopeful . . . it's amazing how hopeful middle age can be.'

He put it down beside him and gestured for the next print, with what seemed like eagerness. I somehow knew he hadn't forgotten the order in which they'd been taken. He was expecting her . . .

When I handed it to him, he smiled a third time, and this time it was a *real* smile. A smile of joy; a smile so joyful that I gave a little shiver down my spine.

'Peggy,' he said. 'Peggy. She was so young. Young and hopeful too. And very much in love. Dear Peggy.'

I saw Phil's hand grip the arm of the sofa. Melanie kept giving little coughs, as if she was trying to dislodge something in her throat. John's face was white and sweating. I think it was starting to get too real for any of them to cope with. I've long known the feeling, from my job.

I handed him the fourth photograph.

'Bendham Woods,' he said. 'We had to be so very careful. I was a married man, with three children. And she was one of my patients. I tried to get her to go to another doctor, but she wouldn't. It would have meant her going into Ipswich by bus . . . She was a lovely girl, but unworldly. Never had a job, just looked after her aged parents till they died. They left her comfortably off, but what kind of life was that for a young woman?'

He looked up; looked at me.

'You're very *calm*, my dear! Are you a policewoman?'

I said, 'Yes, but not from around here. I'm with the Met.'

He said, 'I'm glad.' I couldn't make out whether he meant he was glad I was a policewoman, or whether he was glad I wasn't from round here.

I handed him the last photograph, and he shook his head sadly and said:

'You spotted she was dead, then?'

'I've seen too many . . . '

'Yes,' he said, 'yes.'

Then he looked at me very straight, with those eyes that were too close together.

'What do you want?'

'The truth.'

'Yes, I can see that. But what do your *friends* want?'

He surveyed them calmly. None of them would look at him.

'I expect they want me punished,' he said. 'The world is full of people who want other people punished. I find it a little disgusting. Revenge, I can understand. It's an honest emotion. But people who haven't been harmed themselves, who want people *punished*. What do you think they're up to, eh? I meet people who want the striking miners punished, or unmarried mothers, or drug addicts, or Pakistanis who dare speak up for their beliefs. It's not pretty, my dear. It's not pretty at all.'

He let a long and unbearable silence develop, and watched them writhe.

'Such people never seem to think that life itself can be sufficient punishment. Life and the years that pile up. But no, your friends want me *arrested*. Put on trial. In all the papers, so that all the other people who want to punish can read about my punishment, and have their appetite for punishment satisfied. For a little while. Until they find a new victim.' Then he added, with another straight look at me, 'But I think you only want the truth, my dear. So you shall have it. It's all you will get, I think, because even being arrested would be enough to finish me off. I shouldn't last a week . . . I'm a doctor, and I *know*.'

'Are you guilty?' I blurted out. Because the strangest thing was happening. He was separating me from my friends. It was them I saw as monsters now. I was on his side. Had he some strange magic, that still worked, behind those mottled deathly cheeks and weary burnt-out eyes? Was it the strange magic that had lured Peggy to her death?

'I was guilty – of great heartlessness,' he said. 'And I have been punished for it.'

'Heartlessness is not a crime,' I said.

'Ah, but it should be. It was right that I was punished.' There was no self-pity in his voice, no special pleading. Just . . . I hope when I am old, I can reach that kind of tranquillity.

'What happened?'

He shrugged. 'We fell in love. With all our hearts. I had thought I knew what love was, with my own wife, for my wife and I were always comfortable together, and I loved her till the day she died. But this . . . It was springtime and . . . I don't think we cared if we died for it. We both knew it couldn't last, somehow. It was as if Peggy gathered all her careful life into a great bundle and threw it to me. My only concern was that my wife should not find out and be hurt. So we were very, very careful. We would meet in a quiet spot, and drive to places where nobody knew either of us. That's how we came to pass through Bendham that day.'

'Yes,' I said.

'It may sound very strange to you, my dear, but we never made love – not all the way. We were innocents in those days – not at all like now, when people hop into bed the first time they meet. I know I was an experienced married man, but half the time Peggy seemed more like a daughter. I sometimes think we got more out of holding hands than some of them today get from bed.'

There was a strangled indecipherable grunt from Phil, and he stirred uneasily.

'What happened?' I asked.

Dr Hargreaves gave me another of those straight looks from his faded eyes, ghostly eyes, and said:

'She just died, there in the glade, as I was taking her photograph. We had been . . . extraordinarily passionate, for us. She had a weak heart. I saw her die through the camera viewfinder, as I was clicking the release. I ran to her, tried everything. There was nothing I could do. Except leave her where she lay.'

'*Leave* her?' All John's suppressed rage boiled out in one terrible shout.

'What else could I do? There was nothing I could do

for *her*. She was beyond my aid. And I was a married man and a doctor, with a reputation and a job to lose. My wife would have suffered terribly, if the truth had got out. My children might have starved. Life wasn't a bed of roses in the 1930s, especially for a disgraced and struck-off doctor. I might never have worked again. And I was a *good* doctor.'

He put his face quite suddenly into his hands. I thought he had been taken ill, and touched his arm, but he shook me off.

'It was a solitary spot. They didn't find her body for nearly a week . . . the animals had been at her . . . her face and hands.'

'We've only got your word you didn't kill her,' said John, with a savagery that made me shudder.

'Oh, no,' said Dr Hargreaves, looking up. 'There was a post mortem. And an inquest, of course. She died of natural causes. She had an aneurysm. She couldn't have lasted six months more, the coroner said. I have often wondered if she knew that, instinctively, and that was what made her so desperate for love . . . Here's the details.'

He handed me a brown newspaper clipping, and the same dark innocent face of Peggy stared out at me. But this was a formal studio photograph; she was wearing a silly little hat. The inquest did record a verdict of death from natural causes. There was a coroner's warning about young girls in poor health going for walks alone in lonely places.

'So you got away with it?' said John savagely.

Dr Hargreaves eyed him long.

'I suppose you could say that. My name was never connected with hers. My wife never found out; my children got a good start in life, and still think highly of me.'

John made a sound of disgust in his throat.

'But I don't think I got away with it,' said Dr Hargreaves. 'I was the police surgeon for the area. I was called in to give my professional opinion. I had to help at the post mortem. There was no way I could get out of it.'

'Oh, my God,' said Melanie. 'John, I feel sick.'

'I should take your wife home, sir,' said Dr Hargreaves, 'while you still have her.'

Phil went too. Dr Hargreaves and I stood up. He looked at me, as if from a great distance, as if from the doors of Death itself.

'You are a good policewoman,' he said. 'You'll go far. Because you want the truth. God bless you.' There were tears in his faded eyes now.

'One last question . . . ' I said. Diffidently. Because I didn't want to upset him any more, but I had to know the whole truth.

'Yes, my dear?'

'The camera. How did you come to lose the camera?'

He smiled, a little painfully. 'I couldn't bear to touch it again, after what happened. Knowing what film it had inside it. I wanted to have it developed, so I could have a last photograph of her. But I couldn't risk sending it to any chemist for developing, could I? They look at the prints in the darkroom . . . So the camera hung unused in the cupboard in our bedroom for years. It irritated my wife greatly; that I couldn't bring myself to use it. She wanted photographs of the children as they grew up, like any mother, and she couldn't use it herself – she was frightened of it, it wasn't simple like a Brownie box. In the end, in a fit of rage, she sent it to the church jumble-sale. I never knew a moment's peace after that . . . I didn't even dare to try and trace who'd bought it.'

'Will you be all right?' I asked.

'Whether I live, or die tonight, I shall be all right now. It's such a relief to tell somebody at last. You were as good as a priest in the confessional, my dear.'

I kissed him then; on both withered cheeks. He was so light and frail, it was like kissing a ghost. But a good and faithful ghost.

I have no worries for him. Wherever he has gone.

But I still wonder Who preserved those negatives.

Beelzebub

The Register Office stands like a red-brick Gibraltar amidst the wild ways of Polborough. Five granite steps lead up to doors of solid oak.

It needs those doors. Polborough has always been wild. The inhabitants have that feckless energy and ingenuity that invariably leads to disaster. They do not have the restraining influence of a cathedral, like their western neighbour, Peterborough. They have done too well, too quickly, out of a network of Thatcherite light industry.

Their latest money-making scheme is night-clubs, famed across the Midlands, which disgorge maddened hordes of the drunken young from as far away as Birmingham on to the streets at 2 a.m. Massive street-fights are a growth industry, while the Polborough police huddle together in their fives and tens and hope that real murder is not taking place. Every year the town's fifty-foot Christmas tree is snapped in half by some drunk trying to climb it. Rape is endemic.

Of course, the Register Office suffers. Every Monday morning its windowsills are lined with crushed lager cans, and polystyrene containers full of curry and rain-water. Unmentionable graffiti sprout like mushrooms. The deep shadowy back porch is littered with the débris of sexual passion.

All this is removed by the caretaker before the public can see it. Under the eagle eye of Mrs Parsons, the senior registrar of births, deaths and marriages. (She is convinced she is *senior* registrar; she is the oldest, has been there the longest.)

The Register Office is lucky to have Mrs Parsons, as she is the first to point out. The superintendent is a Mr Brooks, a worried-looking man nearing forty, who has young children at home who always seem to be ailing, and a wife who rings him several times a day to report their symptoms. He does his job, but anyone can see his mind isn't really on it. Mrs Parsons's enduring memory is of him standing with his hand on her door-handle, dark hair dishevelled, spectacles awry and military raincoat unbuttoned, saying:

'I must get home on time tonight, Mrs Parsons. Will you see to things?'

Mrs Parsons had the time and energy to see to everything, having reached that comfortable stage of life when her children were off her hands, and her husband cowed domestically to a mere fetcher-and-carrier. A woman of solid muscular frame, she swam thirty lengths of the baths every Saturday afternoon, and played badminton regularly. Her cheeks were rosy; her red hair, cut sensibly short, seemed to bristle with energy and she found time not only to be churchwarden (*senior* churchwarden) of her parish church, but also organist and head of the Sunday School. She held the theory that most people's troubles were of their own making, and could soon be sorted out by a person with sense.

She ran the Register Office as she ran her parish church. Even in this time of cutbacks, the parquet floor shone like glass. She did fresh flower arrangements twice a week. The smell of wax polish and flowers amounted to an odour of sanctity. The wedding room was freshly painted and curtained to Mrs Parsons's taste. And if her fellow registrars grumbled that their own ceilings were peeling and their chairs uncomfortable, Mrs Parsons told them that in times of financial stringency, sacrifices had to be made.

She had installed a receptionist of so dire an aspect as to cow even such wild inhabitants of Polborough as dared to marry or breed or lose their loved ones. Outrageous requests to use the toilet (reserved for staff only) or the telephone (to contact the undertakers) were crushed instantly.

Of course, even Mrs Parsons could not entirely stem that frenzied flood of desire and delusion that was Polborough. She could not stop forty-year-old divorcees, seven months' pregnant, from getting married in long white wedding-dresses, attended by children of a previous union playing bridesmaid in shocking-pink mini-skirts. She could not stop bridegrooms turning up in ragged jeans and trainers. Or two trampoline champions getting married in their England tracksuits. She could not even stop the proud and pugilistic father of twins registering them as Sugar Ray and Frankie Bruno Rafferty. Or the man who wished to register his son as Thomas H. Lacey.

'What does the "H" stand for?'

'Nothing. Just "H".'

'You can't call somebody just "H".'

'What about Harry H. Corbett then?'

The worst day had been when a prisoner on remand in the local jail came in to get married, accompanied by two warders. Afterwards, of course, the family demanded to have wedding photographs taken on the five steps of the Register Office, just like everybody else. And of course you couldn't expect a man to be photographed in handcuffs on his own wedding day . . . and would the warders, who had been so very kind, like to be in the photograph? In the back row?

No sooner had the large group posed than a car drew up at the kerb. The family closed ranks as tight as a rugby scrum, and the bridegroom was into the car and off before the warders could struggle clear. Only the bride, screeching in marital frustration, had offered any pursuit . . .

Of course, Mrs Parsons was not directly involved. Had she been in charge it would never have happened. But it was she whom the gutter press rang up afterwards, avid for a sensation. She told them coldly that they could purchase copies of the marriage entry, like any other member of the public, and with that, in spite of all their bribes and pleadings, they had to be content.

The frost of Mrs Parsons's disapproval of this incident had not really melted when, one unusually warm afternoon at the end of October, the woman with the baby turned up. Mrs Parsons was not at her best on warm afternoons when there was little business. Her vigorous lifestyle finally caught up with her, and she tended to fall asleep at her desk, which reminded her unpleasantly of her age and her mortality. She would start awake suddenly, with a sense of the world gone awry, and some opportunity missed. It was the nearest she ever got to a sense of guilt.

Mrs Parsons, called to the waiting room by the

receptionist's buzzer, summed up the woman at a glance. Dusty black dress, down-at-heel black court-shoes, no tights. And Mrs Parsons could *smell* the woman, even through the familiar reassuring odour of wax polish and flowers. An earthy smoky smell that followed Mrs Parsons's clicking protesting heels up the polished parquet; that settled comfortably in Mrs Parsons's spotless client's armchair.

The woman had the chaotic voluptuousness of an overgrown cottage garden. Long luxuriant black hair, greasy and held back by an elastic band. Large shapely breasts that must never have known a bra. A broad band of filthy lace petticoat that showed as she crossed her curvaceous but overheavy white legs. A strappy handbag over her shoulder that was no more than a bulging home-made sack of leather. A face full of lovely curves that was somehow both sly and not quite all there.

But it was the baby that really caught Mrs Parsons's attention. The woman was holding it with its face turned away from Mrs Parsons. It looked all of six weeks old and very well grown, but definitely . . . slightly . . . coloured. The odd thing was that Mrs Parsons got the impression it was slightly coloured *green*.

Must be a trick of the light, Mrs Parsons thought. The curtains she had selected for her own personal office were a deep tasteful restful green, and the sun was shining on them pretty strongly, and green light was being gently reflected on to the ceiling. But if the light made the child look green, why did it not make the mother look green as well? Mrs Parsons shook herself free of such distressing fancies, blaming the warmth of the afternoon. Took a firm grip on herself and launched into that registrar's litany of questions that she knew even better by heart than her church's Matins or Evensong.

'Have you come to register a birth?'

'O' course!' The woman looked at her child, affronted, as if to make sure it was still there.

'No, no,' said Mrs Parsons hastily. 'But I have to make sure you haven't come in to register a death, haven't I? I mean . . . someone might come in with their child to register someone else's death, mightn't they?'

The woman looked at Mrs Parsons, as if she thought Mrs Parsons might be slightly mad. Then she said, in a thick Fenland accent:

''Tis birth for this one, though it might be death for some.'

Mrs Parsons had a strong and furious impulse to ask her what the devil she meant; and then an equally strong impulse to draw back from venturing into such a quagmire. The woman's accent was so strong, she might have misheard her. Or it might be some weird old Fenland saying. Stick to the business in hand! At least she now knew she was registering a birth. She drew the relevant draft form towards her and poised her regulation black Biro.

'Are you the baby's mother?'

'O' course!' Again the woman seemed deeply affronted. She gripped her child with a fierce possessiveness. Again, Mrs Parsons felt the need to explain.

'We have to ask, you see. It's our rules. You might have been some other relative . . . ' Then she thought wearily, oh, why bother? She'd never felt the need to justify herself before. What was the matter with her this afternoon? The heat? Or that earthy smoky smell that filled the room and seemed to stir long-forgotten memories from her girlhood, when her world was far less hygienic and well organised than it was now.

'What date was the baby born?'

'Six weeks come Friday.'

What a peculiar way of putting it! Didn't they have calendars where she came from? But, on second glance, probably not. There were tiny bits of dried grass clinging to the woman's bare instep, and what looked like a smudge of cow-dung. Mrs Parsons consulted her own calendar and said briskly, 'That would be the twenty-third of September then?'

'If 'ee say so,' said the woman. 'I'd a ruther it had been All Hallows' Eve, but beggars can't be choosers.' She said it resentfully, as if she'd been cheated.

Why All Hallows, for heaven's sake? Again, Mrs Parsons nearly asked the woman, and then drew back. Get involved in that swamp, you might never get out. Best stick to the road you know.

'Whereabouts was the baby born?'

'Our place.'

Yes, of course, it would be. No nice clean hygienic hospital for this one. Probably in the straw of a byre, among the chickens, if not the pigs.

'And where is "our place"?' asked Mrs Parsons, her voice turning to saccharine over steel.

'Our house. Coveny Lane, Witchford.'

Mrs Parsons looked up sharply. That sounded like a joke, a country joke against a townie. And indeed the woman had a slight irritating smile, hovering round her generous lips. But she said:

'It *was* born there! That's where us were all born!'

But just to make sure, Mrs Parsons went across to consult the relevant ordnance survey map, one of several pinned on her walls. When you dealt with so many idiots, you had to make sure. But indeed, there in the distant Fenland village of Witchford was Coveny Lane. Only there were several small buildings marked in Coveny Lane . . .

'What's your house called?'

'Just our house.'

'What do other people call it?'

Again the woman looked at Mrs Parsons, as if she thought Mrs Parsons slightly insane. 'They do call it Smith's place, I suppose.'

Now Mrs Parsons felt better, as her Biro flew across the form. 'Smith's Place sounds quite historical,' she said pleasantly. 'Is it old?'

'Old enough. The roof do leak. But we do call all the houses "Smith's place" or "Jeffrey's place" or "Policeman's place". 'Tain't a proper name.'

A wave of exasperation flowed through Mrs Parsons. 'I don't suppose it's got a *number*,' she asked. 'To help the postman?'

'Us don't need no number. Postie do know where we do live. Us never gets no letters anyway, 'cept bills an' us saves those to light the fire with.'

So Smith's Place it would have to be. Mrs Parsons just hoped that the General Register Office in London never found out, and sent her the printed reprimand the registrars termed a 'yellow peril'.

'Is the baby a girl or a boy?'

The woman just smiled. The smile came from deep inside her like water slowly oozing up round your feet when you stand in a wet field. As if there was some huge joke that Mrs Parsons would never, never be told.

'Oh, come, my good woman, you must *know*!'

'Oh, he'm *male* all right. Just like his father afore him, and haven't I got cause to know it! But cold as clay his father was, in the dark o' night.' Her slow smile *invited* questions now.

Mrs Parsons said 'Male' briskly, and wrote it down. Then said, equally briskly, 'In what name and surname is the baby to be brought up?'

That was the official form of words, properly to be used. Mrs Parsons knew that some of the other, lesser registrars just said, 'What are you going to call the baby?' She sometimes felt tempted to use those words herself, when the atmosphere was cosy. But it was far from cosy now.

'He's a Smith,' said the woman. 'We'm all Smiths, allus were. Allus have been.'

'And the Christian name?' It just slipped out; Mrs Parsons could've kicked herself. Lots of people weren't Christian these days; they might be atheists or humanists and might object. But she was so anxious to get this registration over . . . and the heat . . . and the smell.

'No, us aren't *Christians*,' said the woman starkly. 'Not Christians, not any of us, never.'

But the awful thing was the child. The child suddenly raising its head from the mother's black shoulder, and turning slowly and looking at the registrar. Black black eyes that were full of steady hate, a hate as cold and desolating as a fen-pool.

Mrs Parsons's mind fled into a flurry of panic, like a

terrified hamster on its wheel. Dear God, babies can't lift their heads at six weeks, nor focus their eyes. They can't understand what you say and they can't *hate*, I can't bear it . . .

After what seemed forever, the child turned away from her and clawed with one tiny green-tinted hand at the mother's black-clad breast. The woman opened her dress with the utmost casualness. The breast was disturbing in its opulence, then it vanished behind the short black hair on the child's head, and there was the ferocious sound of sucking. Mrs Parsons saw the mother wince.

'I'm sorry . . . I'd rather you didn't do that in here,' said Mrs Parsons with much less than her normal certainty. 'It's . . . against regulations.'

'Would 'ee ruther 'ee looked at 'ee then?' asked the woman. ''Tis the only thing that will pacify him, once he's angered.'

The two women stared at each other a long silent time. Duty told Mrs Parsons there were things that should be reported here; the child must be much older than the regulation six weeks' time limit for reporting a birth. Much too big and strong for six weeks, she could see that now. There should be an investigation; the woman had uttered a perjury . . .

But where was the evidence? The child had been born in some hovel, doubtless without benefit of doctor or midwife; born with the help of some wretched old crone who would only back up the mother's lies, like the Fen people always did. The police would be helpless; townie police in the Fen country.

That was what she told herself. But the truth was that she couldn't hold the woman's gaze, so full of untold knowledge. So she dropped her eyes to her form again.

'And the other name? The forename?'

'Beelzebub,' said the woman.

'My dear woman!' Mrs Parsons knew she shouldn't be protesting. Parents had the right to call their children anything they liked. Much worse even than Sugar Ray and Frankie Bruno. Glasnost Graham had threatened before now, and Perestroika Peters been narrowly averted. She had in her desk an official list of approved names, which showed the approved spellings. But that could only be offered as a guide when requested. It could never be used as a weapon, a coercion. But 'Beelzebub'! The name of a devil out of the Bible . . . the woman must have got into a muddle. If she wanted a biblical name, there were lots of nice ones like 'Benjamin' or 'Nathaniel' or even good old Victorian ones like 'Ebenezer' or 'Hezekiah'.

'You can't burden a child with "Beelzebub"!' said Mrs Parsons, her sense of duty overwhelmed by her feelings.

And then, to her horror, as in a dream, she saw the child's head lift and begin to turn towards her again. She could not look away. Again the eyes pierced her very soul with their awful black hate.

'Write!' said the child, in a dreadful, old man's voice.

To support her reeling mind, she leaned forward and clutched the edges of her desk hard. And felt a tiny tickle slide across the skin of her chest. And knew it must be the little silver cross she wore night and day, under her clothes usually. It had slipped from her blouse and was dangling free. Some stray beam of sunlight must have caught the cross, for she saw a flicker of light touch the child's face.

The child flinched, as if burnt, and buried its head in the refuge of its mother's breast again.

Mrs Parsons's mind wriggled vigorously back into reality, as her body wriggled into its foundation garment every morning. Oh, this was all nonsense! Warm afternoon nonsense! She was passing through that awkward time of life; she must go to the doctor and get something! The child must merely have burped and it had sounded like the word 'write'. And its greenness was just the greenness of the light and its size and strength merely . . .

Anyway, her own legal duty was clear. She must write on the form what the mother had told her, and that was the end of it. Her responsibility ended there. So bitterly she wrote the name 'Beelzebub'.

And yet something inside told her she should not have written it. It was another crack in the precious wall of civilisation that held back chaos. There had been so many cracks recently. So many young people not bothering to get married and living in sin . . . a quarter of all the nation's children being born out of wedlock. Those horrible men being tolerated for days on the roofs of prisons, waving their arms and looking like devils from the Pit. Those who should have been on guard were sleeping at their posts, and one day there would be a terrible price to pay . . .

It made her voice a little sharp, a little shrill, as she asked the next statutory question.

'What is the father's full name?'

The woman giggled, a dreadful sound. 'We do just call him "Old Luke".'

'I can't just put down "Old Luke".' It was almost a squeak of outrage. 'The people at General Register Office would never stand for that.'

She glared at the woman, who glared back.

'His full name do be Lucifer. But we do just call him "Old Luke". We don't never see him, you know. Just – he sometimes comes to us, after the dancing, in the dark of night. 'Tis like a dream . . . only you do know he's been, in the morning, you do know that all right! I couldn't sit down for days after . . . and you do know it's he, because he do be as cold as clay.'

Mrs Parsons shuddered, mainly with pity, but not entirely. The customs they still lived by, on the Fen! Who knew? They kept themselves to themselves. Even the police didn't know, let alone the vicars who were supposed to care for their moral welfare. It was a *disgrace*, in this last decade of the twentieth century. This poor young ninny, voluptuous and not quite all there . . . a sitting target for any unscrupulous man after an orgy of drink . . . this pathetic story of Old Luke Lucifer . . . and now she would have the burden of the child, or expect the state to carry the burden of them both, more likely. And most likely it would grow up as much an idiot and a burden to itself as she was . . .

Nevertheless, in accordance with her duties, Mrs Parsons wrote down the father's name.

Luke Lucifer.

And again she knew she shouldn't have done it. There was another crack in the dyke now. In the official records of the nation, in the archives of St Catherine's House, there would be a black lie.

Old Luke Lucifer.

But she had to ask the next question.

'Whereabouts was the father born?'

The woman smiled; an incredulous smile, as at Mrs Parsons's ignorance.

'Why, in the Heavens, before he was cast down!'

Mrs Parsons broke out in a sweat all over, from the small of her back to the palms of her hands. But she controlled herself. She must expect such sweats at her time of life; even if it was not simply caused by the increasing temperature of the room.

But this was the thing she dreaded most. This appalling way even apparently quite sensible people had of leaping suddenly into the totally nonsensical. Even some vicars . . . there had been a visiting preacher two Sundays ago who had gone on and on about the Second Coming. Rubbish about the Blessed being placed on the right hand, and the Damned on the left, while at the same time the Blessed were being lifted up into the air . . . it had made her head whirl, like some spiritual Spaghetti Junction. She had spoken to the preacher quite severely afterwards, saying that in future she would tolerate only sermons about sensible subjects like Inner City Welfare Work, or the Ordination of Woman . . .

'Place of father's birth unknown,' she said out loud, putting a vicious line through the space left for it on the draft form, so great was her exasperation.

She heard the child mutter ominously at its mother's breast, breaking the sound of sucking. But she swept straight on to the next question, even though she knew the answer would be gibberish. She *must* get this business over, and the awful woman out of her Register Office, back to the swamp of ignorance she'd emerged from. It would be like a Cleansing of the Temple.

'What is the father's occupation?'

'He do go about the world, workin' his Will.'

'Commercial Traveller,' wrote Mrs Parsons, with vicious spite.

Again the child rumbled, horrible noises as from a nether pit. Could it sense what she was writing? Or did its nose just need wiping?

She was nearly there now. Only a few more questions, and those were easier, more practical.

'What is your full name?'

'Joan Smith. Us do be all Smiths.' The woman's voice had gone tight; the child's feeding sounded ferocious.

'And what is *your* occupation?'

'I do find things for people, when they've mislaid them. I do charm warts, and mix a cure for the Old Johnny. I can blast a man's crops. I do a lot o' they, afore the village shows . . . '

'Herbal healer,' cut in Mrs Parsons shortly. 'And I think you said that you too were born in Coveny Lane, Witchford?'

'That be right.' The woman sounded not only in pain, but miffed at being rushed like this.

Now for the crunch question. Though as the years passed, sadly it became less and less of a crunch. It was the test of whether the child was illegitimate . . . an 'illy' as they called it in the office.

'What was your maiden name?'

'I told 'ee. Smith I was, and Smith I am and Smith I shall be. Though I don't be no maiden no more.' That came out as a thick snigger.

'So you have never married?'

'Course not.'

'Then I cannot enter the father's name on the birth certificate. Not unless he comes to see me himself.' At this point, Mrs Parsons looked up, putting on her most authoritative official face.

But not for long.

The child fed on. But a trickle of blood descended from the mother's breast, staining deep dark brown into her open black dress.

Mrs Parsons was not, at bottom, uncaring. Her cry of distress for the other woman was loud enough to bring her colleagues running. They gathered in a semi-circle, staring in horror and offering suggestions of cotton-wool and calamine lotion, Savlon and the office first-aid kid.

But the look on the Fen-woman's face held them at bay; she crouched in her chair in the corner like a wild beast protecting her cub.

'Let I be! Let I be! I be all right!'

Mr Brooks looked in, looked harassed, and suggested that an ambulance be summoned. When the suggestion was rejected by all, he fled back to his own office, overwhelmed by such female mystery.

And that led Mrs Parsons to say, 'Leave it to me, ladies. I can handle it.'

When they had all been got rid of, the woman deigned to snatch a large lump of cotton-wool soaked in calamine that Mrs Parsons offered her. She dabbed with it, inside her poor black dress. It seemed to renew some bridge between the pair of them. Mrs Parsons returned to her seat and took charge again.

'Now you do understand? I cannot enter the father's name on the birth certificate unless he comes and asks for it to be put on, himself?'

'He do want his name on.'

'I think you know him better than you make out.' Mrs Parsons smiled a little, as the certainty of her own authority returned.

'Oh, I do know him all right. And his ways.'

Mrs Parsons smiled again, thinking of some great hulking Fen-man, coming cowed into this stronghold of stately authority, sober for once, maybe in his best suit, ill at ease off his own crude ground.

The woman looked at her, almost with pity. ''Ee wouldn't smile if 'ee saw him, missus. 'Ee've seen the son, at six week. Do 'ee really want to see the father?'

And the child on her knee slowly turned its head again and stared at Mrs Parsons, with the pools of hate set in his pale green face. As if in response, the sun went in, outside the window, and the fetid smell grew stronger and more rancid in the over-warm room. Like the smell from the lair of some wild beast.

Mrs Parsons found her own hand clutching the tiny silver cross round her neck.

'Aye,' said the woman. 'That toy in yer hand will scare the young 'un. For a bit. But it won't scare the old 'un, if he comes for yer.'

'I have to do my duty,' said Mrs Parsons, keeping the tremble out of her voice with difficulty.

''Ee won't think of yer duty, if the old 'un comes for 'ee. 'Ee'll do what he tells yer. Only it'll be too late. For 'ee.'

Mrs Parsons thought of the whole august system of

the General Register Office, of the rule of law, of the phone by her elbow, and of the police.

'None o' that will help 'ee, if he comes,' said the woman. 'I told 'ee. He comes in the dark.'

Mrs Parsons thought of the dark. Of getting out of the car in her own tree-lined drive, when her husband wasn't home yet, and her house in darkness. She thought of the dimness of the multi-storey car park, when she had to be in town late in winter. She thought of lying awake in the small hours, when her husband was away on business. She suddenly realised that half the world, half of life, lay in the dark. She'd never realised it was so much, because she'd spent most of it going to the theatre or watching telly, or sleeping. The dark had seemed such a small part of her life . . . Now she realised how much it was there; out across the Fens; between the thin lines of streetlamps, thin as necklaces that might snap.

She came to her crossroads, quite suddenly.

You either belonged to the dark, or you belonged to the light. As you might belong to a hockey team in your youth, or the WI in middle age. The light wasn't a free gift, it was a side you belonged to, an army in battle. As the Bible put it, there were the Children of Light, and the Deeds of Darkness.

And the Deeds of Darkness would never gain an inch, not through her.

She folded her hands together loosely on the desk, almost humbly, and said:

'I'm afraid the father will have to come and see me.'

'Don't blame me. Don't say I didn't warn 'ee.' The woman shot her a look almost of pity. Then walked out in her down-at-heel shoes, clacking off down the corridor, carrying her dreadful child away; into silence.

Mrs Parsons sat on, utterly exhausted. There was no summons, from the receptionist's buzzer, to fetch her to a new customer. Outside the window, the sky darkened and darkened. So *close*! Thunder must be threatening. The fetid smell the woman had left behind seemed to get worse, not better; but Mrs Parsons did not seem able to summon up the energy to cross the room for the air freshener she kept in the cupboard.

Then Mr Brooks was at her door, hand on the door-handle, dishevelled as usual. He must be home on time tonight, would she see to things?

She almost called him back; but he was gone before she could find her voice. Now there were footsteps and echoing female voices in the hall; the rest of the staff were going home.

The big door banged shut, and she knew she was alone. No sound but the far musical drip of the cold tap in the little kitchen at the end of the corridor.

She knew the creature was coming for her. Was she afraid, a small part of her asked?

Oddly, she wasn't. Or only as afraid as she'd been as a child in the bombings of 1940. Tense, worked up, but not afraid. Not terrified. She thought, quite calmly, that this was the best way, here, in the place she knew so well, with her things around her. In the fortress she had defended so long. Better than running away, and then waiting in fear for the dark to come. In the dark she could only grow weaker . . .

In a way, she was glad to end like this. All her life she had been on the fringes of the battle between the light and the dark, good and evil. It made her feel satisfyingly real to be in the centre of the battle at last. She knew her best years were gone; she had a sudden eagerness to spend what was left in a rush. For what she knew was right.

And beyond that, she was filled with a sort of wonder at the creature that would come. If he was real, then she would know for certain that his Adversary, her God, was real too. And it would be a relief, to know that for certain.

There was a vivid flash from the window; then a distant rattle of thunder. Any moment now. She began putting her desk in order . . . the waiting was what was making her drowsy. Her traitorous body was letting down her soul. If the creature caught her dozing . . .

She heard her door squeak as it opened.

'Here's your tea, Mrs Parsons! Mrs Parsons! Mrs Parsons!'

A familiar, unfrightening and indeed female hand was gently shaking her shoulder. She looked up at Mrs Meadowes's freckled face and ginger hair with total disbelief.

'But I heard you go home, Mrs Meadowes!'

'Heavens, no, it's only half past three. I've brought your cup of tea. You must have dozed off. It's ever so close this afternoon. I nearly dozed off myself.'

'Was there . . . a woman in black . . . with a baby . . . a gypsy-looking woman with long hair held back with an elastic band? Come to register the baby?'

The receptionist looked baffled, shook her head. 'We've only had three deaths this afternoon, and two notices of marriage. It's been very quiet. Nobody like that – nobody like that at all. You must have been having a dream . . . '

She gave Mrs Parsons a slightly pitying look that roused all Mrs Parsons's cold wrath. Then said hurriedly, 'Don't let your tea get cold,' and left.

Mrs Parsons stirred her cup of tea, for want of anything better to do. It was then that she saw the draft form, filled out in Biro, in her own handwriting. The name stood out quite clearly.

Beelzebub.

A rage seized Mrs Parsons. She strode to the ordnance survey map on the wall. Witchford was there all right. So was Coveny Lane, with its several buildings marked.

It was Mrs Parsons who left Mr Brooks to lock up and see to things that afternoon. It was Mrs Parsons who drove to Coveny Lane, Witchford, full of rage and yearning, hunting for Old Luke Lucifer, hunting for the last battle, for the truth.

She didn't find any of them, of course. All four buildings in Coveny Lane, Witchford, were large and luxurious modern bungalows. Two of their well-kept gardens contained middle-aged women in smocks and green wellies, up to their elbows in mowing, pruning and weeding. Neither had ever heard of any family called Smith, or seen the woman Mrs Parsons described. Which wasn't really surprising, for Witchford itself wasn't really darkest Fenland at all, but a pleasant prosperous village mainly inhabited by people who commuted to well-paid jobs in Ely. Shaking her head and lambasting herself, back in her car, Mrs Parsons had to admit she'd really always known that.

So where had those creatures come from, the

terrible hating babe, the earthy slut in black, and Old Luke Lucifer who came in the night and was as cold as clay?

There was only one place they could have come from.

Inside herself. They lived there. Always.

For a long minute, Mrs Parsons seemed to teeter on a precipice above endless chasms of darkness, where slimy things coiled and twisted through and round each other, hating, fearing, devouring endlessly, without pity. The truth.

Then she murmured, 'Stuff and nonsense.'

And drove away to get her husband's tea ready.

Blind Bill

Blind Bill's most dreadful day started like any other.

He shifted his position in his garden chair; heard its springs twang and its aluminium feet scrape on the sandstone flags of the sun-trap inside the tall hedge of his front garden.

He heard the gust of wind come round the hill, stirring the leaves of the beech-hanger like the sound of the sea. Then it was running through the cornfield behind his house, whispering soft as a girl. Then it made his telly aerial creak, and leapt upon him, driving his hair across his ear in a teasing tickle. Then it was through the hedge and across the road, making the foil on Mrs Jobson's bird-scarer rattle. And then it was gone, fading down the valley.

A kind warm wind. From the south-west. Driving little white puffy clouds across the bright blue sky. He could feel the cool touch of cloudshadows on his face. But there was more warm sun than cool shadow crossing his cheek.

It could only be August. The smell of his lavender beds was even overpowering the scent of his second growth of roses. The murmuring of bees among the lavender would have made him drowsy, except there were wasps among them. The sound of the wasps' wings was sharper; and wasps were the only thing he feared, here in the safety of his garden.

He checked his table top again, to make sure his wife had left everything there before she went to town. The radio she had given him last Christmas; his fags and matches; the cordless telephone that was his pride and joy. Some time this morning he would ring young Tom at the works. But not yet. He only bothered young Tom in the really lonely times. This morning he had hope of visitors.

And here came the first, regular as clockwork. Heralded by a burst of blackbirds' alarm calls from the fringes of the beechwood. The alarm calls advanced slowly, right down the hedge of the cornfield, sometimes stationary for minutes on end but always getting nearer.

'You won't catch them, you old devil,' he murmured. 'They're too sharp for you. They see you coming. You'll have to make do with cheese, as usual.' He felt for the little strong-smelling packet of cheese on the table in front of him.

The birdcalls rose to a crescendo. There was a strong bitter smell of disturbed nasturtiums from the patch by the compost-heap.

'C'mon, you soft-footed fiend,' said Blind Bill, taking his hands off his lap as a precaution, for claws could be sharp.

He heard the tiny hissing intake of breath, as the cat tensed for its spring. Then four small, painfully heavy paws landed on his legs, and a storm of purring broke out.

Bill stroked the tomcat from its big round head to the

tip of its tail. Its fur was slightly greasy and sticky from too much good living and not enough washing. Tomcats never cleaned themselves the way she-cats did. But Bill liked the faint acrid masculine smell of it.

The cat pushed his stroking hand impatiently with an icy wet nose, demanding its daily cheese.

'Wet nose. You're in good nick then, you black devil.'

He only knew the cat was black because his wife had told him so; it had only come to the garden since his blindness.

But he knew where it had been. He felt the tiny goose-grass burrs called bobby-buttons caught in the fur under its tail.

'You've been down Hutchin's.' Only old Hutchin was a bad enough gardener in the village to let goose-grass run wild over his fences. The cat waited patiently while he dug out the bobby-buttons. Then Bill lifted him and smelt him all over. There was a faint smell of blackberries on his ears; he'd been down among the brambles by the river. Mousing or ratting.

But the overpowering smell was of half-rotten fish and ashes.

'And you've been down to the chip-shop.' The chip-shop bins had notoriously loose lids that blew off in every gust of wind and left the village littered with greasy paper.

The cat nudged again for the cheese. Then Bill heard his paw reaching for the polythene wrapping on it, as it lay on the table top; the soft rustle.

'All right, you old devil, here you are then.'

Afterwards, the cat washed itself, spasmodically.

Bill could feel its neck muscles lunging in the licking rhythm; felt with pleasure the rough tongue stray on to his own stroking hand.

The cat stayed, until his second visitor arrived. Far off, Bill heard the thin tyres of the postie's bike, crunching on the rough cinder track that led up from the village. He was glad it was the sound of Percy, the old postie, the slight puffing because the cinder track was steep.

The young postie, whose name Bill had never discovered, came up the track much more quickly. Bill had never discovered his name because the young postie never lingered, was too embarrassed to stop and chat to a blind man. Just said, 'Morning,' thrust the letters into Bill's hand roughly and went. And Bill would think sadly, ah well, lad, dodge trouble while you can. It'll be your turn one day, when your joints ache, or your wife's run off with another man, or you're going deaf. You'll be glad enough of a kind cup of tea then . . .

Percy always stopped for a cup of tea. The cat stayed while Percy braked and got off with a grunt, and opened the garden gate with a creak. Then, as Bill reached for the big Thermos flask, the cat was gone, and there was a coolish dampish patch on Bill's knee, where the washing cat tongue had been. The cat never stayed when Percy came; it must mistrust him for some reason of its own. Cats were strange cattle, like no one but themselves.

'Nice day, Percy,' said Bill, as the garden chair opposite complained at Percy's weight. 'You've got something for me, then?'

'Three. Gas bill and electric, two of them.'

'I'll leave them for the wife.' Blindness had its privileges. 'What postmark's the other?'

'Luton.'

'Our Barbara's lad. Open it and tell me what he says.'

'Is he the airline pilot?' asked Percy hopefully.

They settled to the long account of the airline pilot's new run to Bermuda, sipping their tea with the respect it deserved.

After Percy, it was only passers-by, who stopped at the gate for a quick or long word. Bill knew every step. Here was Mrs Jobson's heavy tread and heavy panting. It was her day for Willbridge supermarket, of course. She was so tired she nearly went straight in at her garden gate. But conscience smote her, and she put down her heavy bags with a rattle of tins and came across.

'Nice drying day for your washing, Mrs Jobson!'

He took her aback, as he always did. How *could* he know about her washing? Heavens, silly woman; the flapping cracking sound it made as each gust of wind came down the valley was loud enough. And she always washed before going to the supermarket, anyway. What creatures of habit women were . . . He enjoyed teasing her.

'You'd better have it in by three, though. It'll rain by three.'

Again he was rewarded by her gasp of surprise. But she believed him, because he'd always been right before. He could feel the weather fronts coming, as the wind veered west on his cheek and he felt that slight pressure of warm dampness on his skin.

'Eeh, Bill, you're a wizard, a proper weather-wizard. They could do with you on the BBC.'

'They daren't ask me; I'd show up the others too much.'

'Will you be all right, if it rains?'

'I know the way home, Mrs Jobson,' he said, his voice a little sharp suddenly. He could not abide pity.

Thumping wellies and a whiffling-sniffling meant Ted Pocock, retired farmer and confirmed bachelor, and his dachshund Mamie. Mamie always wriggled under the gate and leapt on to Bill's lap, with blunt claws so unlike the cat's. Ted simply leaned on the gate, which creaked heavily under the weight of his massive forearms.

'Morning, Ted!'

'Morning, Bill. Just been for me paper. Nowt in it, as usual. Don't know why I bother buying it.'

Ted was a wonder to Bill. Since his blindness, Bill had used his Russian shortwave radio endlessly to scour the world for news, for the bubbling upheavals of humanity. Yesterday he'd got Radio Kiev, going on about how the Ukrainian Catholics were stealing churches by force of arms from the Russian Orthodox Church. And Radio Melbourne about the increasing use of blackleg aircraft to break the Australian pilots' strike. Sometimes, to Bill, the world and therefore his own head became like a seething cauldron that threatened to explode at any moment. He lay awake at night worrying . . . the world seemed so irreconcilable, true peace further and further away every day.

But no point in mentioning these things to Ted. Even the news from Eastern Europe seemed to pass him by. Ted's crises were so tiny . . . Mamie having worms . . . greenfly on his tomatoes . . . should he chop down the diseased apple tree in his back garden? Ah well, it took all sorts. And Ted was better than nothing. Slowly, carefully, Bill teased a long chat out of him. How's Mamie, how's the greenfly? And all the time Mamie wriggled her serpentine smooth-haired body under his hands, wanting love, begging for approval. What uncertain creatures dogs were, by comparison with the peaceful smugness of cats. Cats knew they were the bee's knees. Restful.

'Aye well, must be off. I'm taking Minnie Harker a few apple logs.' The gate creaked again, as Ted took his weight off it. And Mamie was gone like a thunderbolt from Bill's arms, leaving a gap, a coldness.

Coldness seemed to invade Bill's world. Suddenly, no more sunlight on his cheek. Clouds building. Had he been wrong about the time the rain would come? It would be a scramble, getting everything inside. Telephone into his left cardigan pocket, fags and matches into his right. Radio under one arm, Thermos under the other. And his stick. Lucky his feet knew the way by heart, every treacherous crack in the paving-stones.

But the worst thing was that rain would finish his day so early. Nothing indoors but the radio and the troubles of the world. Or the quiz-games on TV you didn't need sight to play. Bill was good at quizzes. He'd always had a well-stocked mind, but since his blindness, stuffing his brain with new facts was one way of not going bananas.

Indoors, Bill's blindness was a prison cell; radio and telly weren't *real*. Not like being out here, where the dark world still moved, with wind and sunlight, and every sound brought back memories from the time he'd had eyes.

He listened hard. You could tell if the rain was near because sound grew clearer and sharper; and silence more silent. You could *hear* the rain coming, as a hissing whisper two fields away.

No, not rain yet. A slight touch of returning sunlight blessed his cheek. He heard the rooks cawing in the tops of the beech trees and in his mind's eye he saw them, black and whirling as tea-leaves washing down a sink. He heard the sharp burst of a wood-pigeon's wings, snapping off twigs in the covert at the bottom of his own garden. Sounds filled his inner eye with sights, and he was peaceful again.

Still, it was time to ring young Tom, before young Tom went out for lunch. Funny the gifts that blindness brought you. They'd bought him a Braille watch, with raised numerals, but he scorned it. He could tell the time, to within two minutes, night and day. He was listening for the church clock, or his own grandfather in the hall, before they struck. Always caught the tiny clicks that meant the mechanism was getting ready to strike. He heard them now, and grinned to himself in triumph . . .

He picked up the cordless, and tapped out the number faster than a man with sight. Got Rosie, Tom's secretary who had once been his own secretary.

'Morning, Rosie, you starting a cold?'

'No, sir, it was my tea biscuit. It went down the wrong way.'

'How's your young man? He's a Steve at the moment, isn't he?'

'No, sir. Gotta new one. Michael's his name . . . '

Dear gabby red-haired long-legged Rosie. Now she would go into the works canteen for lunch and tell them all how good Old Bill's hearing was, and how he never forgot anything, even if he was blind . . .

'Is Tom there?'

'Just a minute, sir, I'll fetch him.'

Bill listened to the noise of the factory machines. His factory machines; still his. These new phones were wonderful; they picked up everything.

'Morning, Dad! Or is it afternoon?' Tom was a bit puffed. He'd come running to answer the call.

'What're you making this morning? Medium brackets?'

'How did you guess?'

'Lot of drilling going on. And I can't hear the big press working.'

'You're a blooming marvel, Dad!'

It was a game they played every day, and Bill never got it wrong. But then he'd built up the works himself; starting in one rusty Nissen hut, with two men. Now they employed seventy. Trade was flourishing.

For ten minutes they talked over Tom's problems of the day. Disgruntled customers, stroppy suppliers. Bill knew them all. For ten minutes, Bill's mind clicked over like magic, working full out again. Sheer joy. Mind you, he knew Tom saved up problems for him; problems already solved really. He was a good lad.

Then he heard somebody knock on Tom's office door; an urgent voice . . .

Time to go. Get out of Tom's way.

'See you Thursday night, Dad. Sylvia wants to be on your side in Trivial Pursuit again . . . '

Bill smiled wryly as he put the phone down. Oh, he was a hell of a guy at Trivial Pursuit. Didn't need eyes for that. But Sylvia was a good lass; he was glad young Tom had married her.

They were all good. It was all good.

Then the despair hit him, like it always did. All good; but he'd give it all away, just to have two eyes again. He'd be happy to start all over again with nothing, in that rusty Nissen hut, even at the age of sixty-three. To be rid of the dark. To be rid of being a useless old bugger that everyone was kind to . . . to be of use again, in the world.

For a long while he sat, hands clenched, deaf as well as blind to the world around him. He was a tornado caught in the narrow prison of his own body.

In the end, it passed. It was a thrush singing that broke through first, a lovely liquid sound that soothed him like a glass of water soothes a fevered child. Then the tits going psi-psi-psi. Then a yellowhammer calling:

'A little bit of bread and no *cheese*.'

His hands suddenly relaxed. His mind ventured out, his inner eye riding on the back of his ears, like an old witch riding her broomstick. He smelt again the lavender, and the roses. New sunlight stroked his unclenching hands like a mother.

Be grateful for what you've got, lad. Anything else is hell.

It was nearly one, when he heard the voices. A girl's voice, a boy's voice. Two pairs of feet coming up the cinder track, slowly, not hurrying, out for a walk.

Love's young dream.

Bill smiled, remembering his own courting days, back in the fifties. He listened to the low voices without shame. He was a terrible eavesdropper these days, though no one would ever accuse him of being a Peeping Tom.

The girl had a soft timid voice. Somehow he knew she would be small, small and dark, with a shy smile that would be worth waiting for, worth coaxing out of her. He was entranced. His wife's voice had never been like that. Monica's had always been loud. He had heard her laying down the law to somebody, before he even saw her for the first time. Nobody was ever left in any doubt what Monica thought about *anything*. When he had first told her she was beautiful, she'd said, 'I'm not bad. All bum and no boobs, like most English girls.' He had never been out with a girl who was shy, who needed coaxing.

He was so entranced that he was slow to notice the boy's voice.

It was a wrong voice. Rough, uneven. It didn't fit in with the girl's voice. It kept breaking through what she said like a hammer, a hammer in the hands of . . . an untrustworthy fool. In his time running the works, he'd heard many such voices and they'd always meant trouble. They belonged to lads who were constantly late for work, knocked off early, would be caught mooching off to the toilets for a smoke twenty times a day. Lads who caused fist-fights in the workshops, who bullied new kids, painting their private parts with tar, half-drowning them in tanks of oily water, once almost fatally. Louts who took the live rats from the humane traps and tortured them in the works furnaces. Louts who, in the end, got caught sneaking out of the works gate with stolen copper wire coiled round their body under their shirt. No-good wrong 'uns.

And he'd heard the same voices in court, when he'd sat as a magistrate. Muggers, attempted murderers, would-be rapists . . .

What was a girl like that doing out with a boy like that?

They paused outside his gate. He was quite sure they hadn't noticed him sitting behind the cover of the hawthorn hedge.

'What we coming up here for, Trev?' The girl sounded a bit nervous. Perhaps she was starting to get his number.

The lad chuckled, not very pleasantly. 'Oh, we'll just sit down in the cornfield an' watch the birds an' the bees . . . '

'We haven't got nothing to sit on. I'll get my best dress dirty!'

'We can sit on my anorak.'

'But it'll get all grass stains . . . and it's new.'

'Grass stains won't show on this colour. 'At's why I bought it . . . '

'I'm not snogging or anything. There's too many houses round.'

'Bugger them. This 'as always been a lovers' lane. When I was a kid I used to come 'ere to watch the courting couples . . . you didn't 'arf see some sights.'

'Oh, you are awful. Didn't the fellers see you an' come an' bash you?'

'See *my* head in a cornfield? With hair this colour?'

'I like your hair. I like running my hands through it.'

'Washed it last night, special for you.' That should

have sounded touching. But there was a note in the voice that made the listening Bill shudder.

There was a long awkward silence, outside the hedge. Then the girl said, 'Look at them apples on the tree. Never saw apples growing like that before. Aren't they pretty among the leaves?'

'D'you want one, then?'

'No! They belong to the people in that house. They might be watching.'

'Bugger them. I'll get you one.'

There was a small grunt of effort, then a wild commotion of leaves from the apple tree set into Bill's hawthorn hedge. Then the sound of feet returning to the ground with a thump.

Bill frowned in puzzlement.

'No, don't, Trev. They're too high up anyway.'

The frown on Bill's face increased.

'Bugger that. I said I'd get you one, an' I will.'

There was another grunt of exertion, another massive rustling among the leaves, and an ominous crack from one of the branches.

'Oh, Trev, you're breaking it. Leave it, *please*!'

'Third time lucky. Here goes.'

A total fury of thrashing leaves, creaking and cracking, and then a loud snap. And the sound of apples thudding on the ground.

'That's settled its hash. Here yar. One two three four five six seven. That'll keep you goin' till teatime. Don't say I never give you nothin'.'

'But you've broke that branch. Can't you tie it up again?'

'Bugger them. Snobs. Why should they have all the

bloody apples? Don't have no apple trees round where I live. Not even bloody streetlamps. Sod them!'

Bill sat and shook with fury. The odd apple taken he never minded. Human nature. But *seven*. And a broken branch. He leapt up to deal with the young thug . . .

And then remembered he was blind. And this was 1990, not 1950. And that was the kind of voice that would knock a blind man down and kick him where he lay, and Bill knew it. He stood very still and quiet, trembling.

The footsteps and the voices faded, and Bill sat down in his chair again, with a thump, breaking out in a sweat of relief that they were gone. He had done the sensible thing, and he felt totally humiliated. Then a mad spurt of rage hit him and he wanted revenge. He'd ring up the police and report them. The local Panda would soon catch the young lout, because the cinder track didn't lead anywhere . . .

But even if they caught him . . . Bill hadn't seen him break the apple tree, only heard him. And hearing wasn't evidence. And, anyway, he'd only get a fine for vandalism, even if he was found guilty. And then the young lout would come back for revenge. Throwing bricks through the windows after dark. You couldn't win, these days. As a magistrate he'd seen too often what happened to the elderly who got across the criminal young.

Bill sat fretting at the way the world had changed. Fretting for himself. Until a new thought hit him.

A lout like that, who smashed apple trees; who would beat up a blind man . . . and Bill was letting him go off into the depths of the fields with an innocent young girl . . .

The tones of the yob's voice ground through Bill's memory again and he just knew something terrible was going to happen. As sure as he knew the church clock was just about to strike one; as sure as he knew the rooks had settled again in the top of their tree; as sure as he knew young Tom was making medium brackets today.

But who would believe him? Blind men were second-class citizens. Blind men had to work very hard at being sensible and down-to-earth at all times, or people thought their blindness was driving them potty. The police would laugh at him. His wife would tell him not to be stupid. Even young Tom would be . . . gentle, understanding . . . would humour him . . . and do nothing and begin to pity his poor old Dad.

But the girl had sounded so nice, gentle, innocent. He'd have liked to have her as a daughter, now that Hermione was grown up and the all-too-sensible mother of three.

What could he *do*?

Only wait. And listen. Listen as he'd never listened before.

He settled himself solidly and comfortably, so his chair wouldn't creak as he breathed. He practised breathing silently, only a stray fleck of phlegm in his throat set up an irritating whistle that sounded as loud and distracting as a factory hooter.

Some say the blind are given extra-powerful hearing to make up for their blindness. More sensible people say that the blind simply learn to concentrate every ounce of their grey matter on their ears. Whichever it was, Bill's mind went out and out into the country-side, riding on the back of his ears.

He heard Mrs Jobson turning off her kitchen tap. It always squeaked. He heard a tiny pattering in the leaf-filled ditch. A mouse . . . and something bigger after it, for he heard the mouse's tiny death-squeak . . .

And then with an inward groan of agony, he heard the approaching sound of his wife's car, as she changed down to take the slope up the cinder track. He loved Monica dearly, but she was the noisiest person in the world. She trod the earth in her sensible shoes like a colossus, slammed cupboard doors, drew curtains so fast their runners sounded like a rocket taking off, thumped cushions to make them plump again.

The car revved noisily, backing into their parking space. Its door slammed. Monica grunted as she hefted the laden Sainsbury's carrier bags, which clinked and rattled and glugged. She might as well have been a thunderstorm.

'Still sitting in the garden? It's going to rain. I'll give you a hand with your things . . . just let me dump these groceries.'

'I'm not coming in yet,' he snapped. 'It's not going to rain for hours.'

'Suit yourself. You just look so silly sitting in the garden when the sun's gone in.'

'Leave me be, woman!'

The old tone of command had crept into his voice; the tone he had never used since he went blind. The man who was boss in his own house. From her silence, he knew she was wondering about him, watching him, trying to decide if there was really something the matter, whether she should ring young Tom, or fetch the doctor.

Then she said again, 'Suit yourself. I'll be making lunch in ten minutes . . . '

'I don't want any lunch. I want to stay out here.'

She sighed in exasperation, and clinked and glugged off through the front door. She would return to the attack when she had put away the shopping. Meanwhile, thank God, the depths of the house muted her never-ending noise; and he listened again.

Damn it, the wind was getting stronger. Sending the first leaves of autumn to hit the cinder track with sharp taps, making the telly aerial creak more often, and whining a low mournful note in the telephone wires. Damn damn damn, was everything against him?

And then he heard it. The scream. If Monica had been there, she would have told him not to be silly; that it was a bird, or a stoat with a rabbit. But he knew all the bird-calls and he'd heard a stoat kill a rabbit, and this was neither. It was a human, female scream. Cut off short.

And not just any old scream. Living on a lovers' lane he knew all the kinds of female scream. The scream of sexual excitement, the scream of drunken hilarity, even the screams of two girls fighting each other. And it was none of these. It was a scream of pure terror, cut short. And not repeated, though he waited and waited.

And then he heard the running footsteps. Men's footsteps; no woman could run that fast outside a running track. Male footsteps running for their life, coming nearer. From up the cinder track. A short high-pitched panting, that had something of terror in it.

The footsteps passed the gate. And as they did so, they slapped down on the only piece of track that was not cinders. Three huge sandstone paving-slabs that Bill had laid himself, so proudly, six years before. They slapped down on the sandstone with a particular kind of slap, that Bill knew well.

And then they were gone.

And Bill's moment of decision had come. He had so little time, before Monica came out again and swept all his ideas away with cries of 'Nonsense'.

He picked up the cordless phone and dialled 999.

Thank God it was a policewoman who answered. They were much better listeners than policemen.

She took him seriously. 'We'll send a car to check immediately, sir. Cinder Lane, Welbury. Have you any description of the young man?'

'Short,' he said. 'Less than five foot six. Long blond hair, newly washed. Wearing trainers, denim jeans and a dark anorak, probably green. She called him "Trev".'

'Thank you, sir. And you are Mr Millfield on Welbury 236. We'll be in touch as soon as we know anything, Mr Millfield.'

God help me, he thought. If I'm wrong they'll have me down for a nut-case.

Then Monica came out, and said in dire, no-nonsense tones:

'Lunch!'

He went in like a lamb.

He picked at his lunch, in a way that made Monica take little snorts of protest. He heard the Pandas coming when they were fainter than the chirping of the sparrows in the garden.

One sped by, up the cinder track.

'What the devil's going on?' asked Monica, rushing to the front door.

He said nothing, just trembled inwardly. Afraid they would find something; afraid they would find nothing.

Ten minutes later, they heard the ambulance coming, siren blaring.

'For Heaven's sake,' shouted Monica, dropping her knife and fork and tearing out again. A vast feeling of relief swept over him, that he hadn't proved a blind useless old fool. And then he squashed it down savagely, thinking of the girl, the poor child . . .

'I'm going to see what's up,' shouted Monica from the front door.

He huddled down into his chair, feeling old and ill.

Much later, after he had dozed off in his armchair, thinking he was not as young as he used to be, Monica opened the lounge door and said, in dire tones:

'There's a policeman to see you.'

'Inspector Ambleside, sir,' said a very policemanly voice that was also full of respect. Bill turned his head to the sound, and managed an exhausted smile.

'Take a seat, Inspector. The big ones are comfortable.'

Heavy serge whispered against uncut moquette as the Inspector settled himself.

'You'll be pleased to know, sir, that we found the young woman in the cornfield where you said. She was bleeding heavily but still alive. I've just heard from the hospital that she's going to live. But she would've died, if we hadn't found her . . . '

'Good,' said Bill.

'And we got the man. In fact we found him first. Walking along the main road, bold as brass. Your description fitted him perfectly. All you'd missed was the white stripes on the sleeves of his anorak. And he was so shaken at being nicked he's singing like a canary. Nasty bit of work – collapsed like a paper bag the moment we laid hands on him.'

'Good. I'm very glad,' said Bill.

'The only thing is, sir . . . your wife says you're as blind as a bat. If you'll pardon the expression . . . '

'Yes.'

'So how the heck did you do it?' The Inspector's incredulity burst out of him, making him sound like an affronted schoolboy.

'I listened, Inspector. I heard the thump of trainers on sandstone. I heard the noise denim jeans make, when the legs rub together. I heard the noise nylon sleeves make, when the arms rub against an anorak. And what colour hair won't be noticed in a cornfield? And what colour of anorak won't show grass stains?'

'Yes, I can see all that, sir, though I marvel at it. But how did you know he was so *little*?'

'He had to jump for the apples outside my gate, Inspector. Jump hard. But I go out to feel those apples every fine morning in life. And I can reach them just by raising my arm. But then, I'm six foot three . . . '

'He's only a little 'un,' said the Inspector. 'Five foot three at the most. Evil little bastard. How did you know he was a wrong 'un?'

'Just his voice. Like I know you're a right 'un, Inspector. As well as a big 'un.'

'How . . . ?'

'I know you're tall, because I heard your voice go

funny, as you ducked under that doorway. And I can tell you're big, because of the way that chair creaked, when you sat down.'

'Strewth . . . you should be on the force, sir. You could teach some of my lads a bit about observation.'

'Comes of being as blind as a bat, Inspector. It's lucky your girl didn't know I was blind, when she took my call . . . '

The Inspector sighed deeply, as if he suddenly had all the cares of the world on his shoulders.

'Don't take it to heart,' said Bill. 'I think from the sounds in the kitchen that you're about to be offered a cup of tea.'

Charlie Ferber

At Christmas-time, in my grandmother's house, the ghost cats return.

You never see them straight and solid; only a flicker in the corner of your eye, that vanishes behind a chair and never reappears, however hard you search.

I thought at first it must be a trick of the light, in the corner of my spectacles. Then I started to wonder if I was going peculiar.

But her living cats, the warm furry bundles I so often picked up to cuddle, seemed to see them too. Even when I couldn't. They'd be sitting peacefully on the hearthrug, then suddenly they'd prick their ears and their eyes would follow something around the room, and then they'd prook a greeting or a mild challenge. As if they knew some of the ghost cats, but not others.

I would hear these soft welcoming or querulous outbursts on the stairs, or in the upper corridor, or in the bedrooms overhead. But only at Christmas. The rest of the year, the house was peacefully silent.

Finally, I asked my grandmother. She sat down in her chair and smiled.

'Of course they're there.' She gave me a wondering look. 'So you see them too! That makes you a bit special. Nobody else sees them, you know. Not your mother; nor your father.'

The way she said it made me sorry for my mother and father.

'Why do they come?'

'Because they've been happy here. They just come back to say hello at Christmas.'

'Are there . . . a lot?'

'Dozens. I've had cats all my life. They die, no matter how much you love them. A lot died on the road outside, while they were still quite young. So they come back to see me . . . '

For a moment, her face was sad. Then she decided it was a sadness she wouldn't drag me into. So she smiled again, her face lit up, and she said:

'But there's one ghost cat you'll never see. The ghost of Charlie Ferber.'

'But he was a man,' I said. 'He was . . . '

'He was a cat as well. My first cat.' She mused, with her finger at her fine pale cheek. 'Shall I tell you about him? I've never dared tell anyone else. Your mother would lock me up in the loony-bin.'

'Let her try!' I said. But I knew she was only joking.

'Well, as you know, Charlie Ferber was a man first. A magician, a very famous magician from America who did tours of the English music-halls before the war. A friend of my father's, though God knows where my father met him. He wasn't really my father's sort at all. My father was in the City, a real sobersides, as they all were then. Bowler hat and black coat and striped trousers and an umbrella rolled so tight it looked like a sword.

'Charlie was always . . . a bit flashy. Suits a little loud; fond of wearing a straw boater in summer. He and my parents were as unlike as chalk and cheese. But he was world famous, you see. I suppose my parents were flattered; *and* all their stodgy friends.

'I'll never forget the first time he came to tea. He said, "Oops, excuse *me*," to my young brother, and reached into his ear and produced a silver dollar, just as my mother was pouring out. Gave my brother the dollar too, saying it truly was his and he should keep it in a safer place. I could see my parents were none too pleased . . .

'Then there was my twelfth birthday party. All the dreary adults came to your birthday party in those days and sat around talking, the men about stocks and shares and the women about their awful servants. And the children came wearing their best clothes and hardly dared move, even when we were playing hunt-the-thimble.

'Well, that's how it was, until Charlie turned up. He'd brought me a doll from New York that was nearly as big as I was. I'd stopped playing with dolls by that time, of course, but I'd taken to collecting them – I still have most of them. Anyway, this was the ultimate American doll, which had all kinds of wonders for those days. Big blue eyes that opened and shut as you tilted it. It said "Mama" too, and you could give it a drink, and then it would pee. All this Charlie explained to the assembled gathering, and the grown-ups smirked and sniggered behind his back.

'Then he nearly started a riot with his silver-dollar trick, and finally he sat down at the grand piano without as much as a by-your-leave and started a singsong, all the latest numbers. He had a lovely voice with a laugh in it, a bit like Danny Kaye's. He even looked a bit like Danny, lean and comical, with those shining blue eyes.

'All my friends loved it. But their parents couldn't get them away fast enough. He was always better with kids than adults, Charlie. Just a big kid himself in many ways. That's why the public loved him.

'I thought that party would be the end of a beautiful friendship. Certainly my parents never asked him round again to meet their friends. But he kept on turning up at the house during the day, when my father was away earning pennies in the City, and I think my mother had a soft spot for him. Certainly she let him take me out for day-trips, providing I was always home by five. I think she'd have liked to come herself, but didn't quite dare.

'Oh, that was a fabulous summer holiday! We only did the usual London things, like rowing on the Serpentine, or going to the Natural History Museum or the Zoo. But Charlie could make anything hilarious. On the Serpentine, he'd slip one arm out of the sleeve of his jacket, pretending to be a one-armed man. Then he'd row the boat with only one oar, going round and round in circles, casting desperate glances about, as if appealing for help. And all the English people were too embarrassed to offer help . . . *so* embarrassed! Until we couldn't take any more and collapsed in giggles.

'And at the Natural History Museum, he'd walk around like a dinosaur, pretending to be Tyrannosaurus Rex, till the attendants nearly threw us out.

'And at the Zoo he'd square up to the old male orang-utan. And the orang-utan would pull faces, and Charlie would pull them back at him, then the orang-utan would scratch under his armpit and so would Charlie. Then the orang-utan would beat his chest and bellow and Charlie . . . he drew quite a crowd.

'But the best was our rides on the elephant. Charlie would bend down and whisper some Indian words in the elephant's ear, and the elephant would suddenly turn round and go back the way it had come, without warning, leaving its keeper tearing his hair.

'Once, on a bus going home, Charlie tapped a man on the shoulder and said: "Sir, why do you always carry golf-balls in your hat? It's a most unsafe practice." And then he whipped off the man's bowler hat, and there were two new golf-balls nestling inside.

'The man didn't know what to say (for Charlie kept his face utterly straight). He was silent for a long time, then he said: "Very decent of you to point it out, I'm sure," and went all red and got off the bus at the next stop. After that, we couldn't see a man in a bowler hat without having hysterics.'

My grandmother was silent for a long time, smiling to herself. Then she said,

'I fell in love with Charlie Ferber that summer. I was only twelve, and he wasn't all that much younger than my father. But I fell in love with him, and I think he must have fallen in love with me. He never kissed me. All my father's other friends thought they had the right. My mother would say, "Kiss your Uncle Frank good-bye" or "Haven't you got a kiss for poor old Uncle Ned?" and all they ever were to me were bristly faces like sandpaper. But Charlie never kissed me. Never even held my hand. But he called me his princess, and treated me like a princess. We used to have tea at

Claridge's and the Ritz, and the waiters fell over each other to serve us, because they all knew who Charlie was.

'And then . . . paradise came to an end. Perhaps Charlie grew careless. One day we went to feed the ducks in St James's Park. I suppose some friend of my father's who worked in Whitehall saw us laughing and fooling together in a world of our own; and told him.

'I looked out of my window the next Saturday morning and saw Charlie running up the front steps of our house in Pimlico. He looked up and waved to me and smiled. I wondered at his coming . . . when my father was at home.

'Then all hell broke loose downstairs. I could hear my father shouting, and Charlie trying to reason with him and my mother trying to break in to restore peace, and then my father shouting some more. And I knew from the hate in my father's voice that it was the end . . . I didn't even try to go downstairs and say goodbye to Charlie.

'I saw him coming down our front steps again, putting on his boater. Then he looked at the windows of the room downstairs, where my father was still shouting at my mother, and he gave them such a look my blood ran cold.

'It's not enough to say Charlie loved like a child and hated like a child. It was worse than that.

'The only thing I can liken it to is the cheetah a friend of mine kept as a pet. She used to bring it to parties. It was beautiful beyond words and beautifully trained. Let itself be stroked like an ordinary cat, except it was much more gracious. Would even feed from your hand . . . vol-au-vents and cocktail sausages. Its eyes were gentle, benevolent like a god's . . . until it met one clod of a man who couldn't resist jabbing his fist in its face and making fun of it. Then its eyes changed, and it opened its mouth and showed the most terrible teeth . . .

'Well, Charlie's eyes changed like the cheetah's eyes and I realised he was not quite like other men.

'He was a magician. Like King Arthur's Merlin had been a magician. He didn't just do tricks; he could really work magic.

'Then he looked up and saw me, and his face cleared and he gave me a last grin, and made a sign he often used, to tell me things were going to be all right.

'Then he walked clean out of my life.

'I was pretty upset. Even more upset after I'd been summoned downstairs. I was told I was never to see Charlie again. Or ever mention his name. If he passed me in the street I wasn't even to look at him; I was to cross the street to avoid him.

'All this I was made to swear on the big black family Bible.

'I cried, and lashed out and told my father I hated him, and that I loved Charlie. I hurt my father all I could, for what he'd done to Charlie and me. I was only twelve, but you can hate when you're twelve, can't you? More, perhaps, than you can ever hate later.

'It certainly left my father white and shaking. But he only sent me up to my room for the rest of the day and I spent it crying. Not only with hate, because I didn't *really* hate my father then. More from fear, because Charlie Ferber was a magician, and I'd seen that look on his face.

* * *

'At lunch the following Saturday, when things were just beginning to mend between my father and me, there was a ring at our bell. My mother went to the window, to see who could be calling at such an unreasonable hour. She said there was a delivery van from one of the West End stores.

'Then the maid brought in a basket, the kind you carry pets in. My mother opened the basket, and inside was a Siamese kitten.

'Of course there was a great hoo-ha.

' "Who can have sent it?" asked Mother.

' "Some stupid mistake," said my father. "Get the maid to run after the delivery man and get him to take it away."

'But the kitten knew it was no mistake. It staggered towards me, its blue eyes fixed on mine in pure adoration.

'And its eyes were the same shining blue as Charlie Ferber's. I cuddled it, as the argument raged above my head.

' "It's no mistake," said my mother. "Our address, Millie's name. It's a present for Millie."

' "Totally unsuitable. It must be sent back."

' "But we don't know who sent it . . . and here's its pedigree. Must have cost the earth, from a shop like that." My mother was perhaps too impressed by money and pedigree, in people as well as animals.

' "You know very well who sent it!" raged my father. "Only one man would be fool enough to send it. It's not even her birthday or Christmas . . . it's out of the question. It's going back."

'He tried to grab the kitten off me, but I backed

away. The kitten cowered as the shadow of his large hand fell upon it.

'I glared up at him, and saw his white collar and regimental tie, his bristly large-pored face and the silly little thin dark moustache he was so proud of, his Brylcreemed hair and the brown hotness of his eyes. And in that moment he was no longer my father; only a big brutal stranger who wanted to steal from me everything in my life that was beautiful and happy.

' "If you take it away," I said, "I shall go away too."

'He laughed out loud. How could a twelve-year-old run away? But I went on glaring at him and suddenly he stopped laughing.

'For there *are* ways a twelve-year-old can go away. She can go away inside herself and never come out again. And the years will roll away, and soon she will be twenty, and then she can do what she likes.

'I saw the first flicker of doubt in his eyes; the first flicker of fear. And then I knew even a tyrant needs to feel loved.

'My mother broke into his silence.

' "What harm can it do? A little cat?"

'Little did she know . . .

' "Oh, do as you like," shouted my father, and left the room, his lunch unfinished, the cheese and biscuits lying uneaten on his plate.

'Mother worked hard to pour oil on troubled waters. She cuddled me, and stroked the kitten's head. The kitten didn't seem to mind *her* hand . . .

' "What're you going to call him?"

' "Charlie!"

'She flinched and closed her eyes, seeing further torments ahead.

' "Don't you think Charlie's rather a silly name for a cat?" she said at last. "Why don't we call him 'Chuck'? Like in that rhyme, 'Charlie, Charlie, Chuck, Chuck, Chuck'?"

'So Chuck he became, to my mother. I called him nothing, when my father was around, but Charlie to everybody else. My father only ever referred to him as "that blasted cat of yours".

'And so, for a while, peace was restored.

'My father said the kitten must live in the kitchen with the servants. If he ever saw him upstairs, he would "chuck" him out of the front door!

'Charlie bided his time, almost as if he knew. He seduced the kitchen staff on sight with his taking ways. He never disgraced himself, never broke anything, even in his wildest kitten scampers, never stole food. He didn't have to. He dined on cream and chicken and the best cuts of roast beef, and grew rapidly.

'Whenever I went down to see him, he was with one of them. Curled up in Cook's lap, if she was taking a break. Or sitting on the table watching the kitchen maid chop vegetables, as solemn as a little Christian, as she said. But if he often made them jealous of each other (and it was terrible, the way they tempted him with titbits, to be their special favourite), he never made them jealous of me. In fact they praised his fidelity to me.

' "Here's your mistress," they would call to him, and to me they would say, "Here's your little boy-friend!"

'The first time he broke through their green baize

door, he completed the total seduction of my mother. He walked straight to her, in an undeviating line, putting one foot exactly in front of the other in a very precise and gentlemanly way. A yard off, he sat down and stared at her intently, as if to say:

' "Are you my friend?"

'And when she said, "Hello, Chuck," he leapt into her lap and spent the rest of the afternoon there, as if there was no place in the world he'd rather be.

'She sat long, stroking him; she even let me pour out our afternoon tea, so that she would not disturb his sleep. And finally, when she heard my father's step outside, she got up in a great panic and opened the door for Chuck herself, whispering softly, "Run, Chuck, *run*!" And then turned to greet my father, as the front door opened, with all the gushing guilt of a wife who has spent the afternoon with her lover . . .

'I wasn't jealous. I just marvelled at Charlie's skill in conquering the defences that my father had placed around me. From that day on, he roamed the house freely, passing through the green baize door as if it no longer existed. The only one who never saw him was my father. It was not that Charlie was *afraid* of my father; he never panicked when he heard his step; he had a hundred hiding-places, some contemptuously visible to anyone who really had eyes to see. I have known him crouch in the niche on the staircase, and watch coolly while my father passed within two feet of him. But my father was all mouth and no eyes. I remember thinking that if Charlie had been a tiger and my father the tiger-hunter, my father would have long since been dead and eaten.

'Quite soon, Charlie was spending every night in

my bed. When I got to my bedroom, he would be already there, lying so regally on the silk bedcover that he looked as if he owned the room and owned *me*. At half past nine, when my father came up to say good night, Charlie would slide under the bed at the last possible moment . . .

'Bedtime had been the time in the old days when my father and I had been closest. He had a great passion for reading me *Winnie the Pooh*. (The books were new then, and all the rage.) I'm afraid I grew weary of them, long before my father did. But I would listen patiently, for his sake. That was while I still loved him; when even the horrid smell of whisky on his breath didn't matter, or the roughness of his bristles.

'But the silent listening presence of Charlie under the bed utterly destroyed our closeness, though I still faithfully went through the motions. Charlie thought my father a great blundering ludicrous fool, and he made me see him that way too.

'I, too, came to feel almost like a guilty wife with a concealed lover.

'My real alarm about Charlie the cat began one day, when I took out his pedigree for the hundredth time, to read his grand oriental name, and the even grander oriental names of his ancestors. That hundredth time, a tiny slip of thin paper came out with it; a slip I had never realised was there.

'All it said was: "He will keep you safe until I come. Charlie Ferber."

'I looked at Charlie the cat. He was full-grown by then, but in spite of all his titbits there wasn't an ounce of fat on him. He was long and slim and muscular, as Charlie the man had been. He was a mocker of human folly, like Charlie. And his blue eyes surveyed me so sharply, and I could not tell what was in their depths.

'I took in a deep shuddering breath.

'Charlie Ferber had been a magician; and magicians were dangerous.

'The first occasion when Charlie kept me safe for Charlie was my fourteenth birthday, which was quite different from my twelfth. Father had decided it was time I was introduced to the right kind of boy.

'The right kind were the sons of my father's friends. Didn't matter if they were spotty or fat, show-offs or spiteful little sadists. If they were the sons of friends of my father, they were all right.

'We played vaguely sexy games, including Murder. I'd never found out why it was called Murder. It was really only hide-and-seek, played all over our large house; but in pairs, a girl and a boy together. I mean, spending a lot of time hiding in a small dark space with a boy . . . on the other hand, if you didn't feel like it you needn't do anything but whisper and giggle pleasantly. In any case, you couldn't go too far, because at any moment the searchers might reveal you to the light of day . . .

'I worked hard at being the gracious little hostess, making sure the people who were going off in pairs didn't actively hate each other. I worked so hard at this that I didn't at first realise I hadn't a partner myself. Which was odd, because my mother had made sure we had equal numbers of boys and girls . . .

'And then my partner showed up, saying he'd just

been to comb his hair; and my heart sank. His name was Marc de Leeuw, and his mother was French and caused raised eyebrows in my father's circle. And you just knew that Master de Leeuw had seen too much and heard too much. A bad case of wandering hands, the sort who put his tongue in your mouth, my friends said. For all his pale blond good looks, I'd as soon have been locked in a cupboard with a boa constrictor. But my mother said:

' "Come along, dear, don't keep your guests waiting!"

'The de Leeuws were filthy rich, and my father did business with them, so off I had to go. I tried suggesting hiding behind doors, in the open. But Marc was an old hand at Murder, and dragged me by main force into the upstairs linen cupboard.

'I was considering whether to grab one of his wandering hands and bite it hard, when I felt a soft brushing against my leg. I nearly screamed my head off, and to hell with my father's Gilts and Equities . . . then I realised the touch was furry.

'I felt Charlie rear up gently against my leg, then transfer himself to Marc's. Then his body tensed and his front claws went in.

'Marc's scream brought them running from all over the house. I think they really thought a genuine murder had occurred.

' "Blasted cat," yelled Marc. "Look – I'm *bleeding*. The damned animal should be put down. He's a menace to human life . . . "

' "You *trod* on him," I lied, clutching the condemned criminal to my bosom. "Siamese are very highly-strung and sensitive!"

'After that, all my worries were social ones, like was there enough raspberry jelly to go round.

'Otherwise, I worked hard at my studies. This wasn't being a swot; this was *survival*. I knew my father's plans for me. I was to become a dim debutante and curtsey nicely to the Queen, and go to lots of balls and end up married to some rich drip and spend the rest of my life breeding children (and dogs, if I was lucky enough to get a rich drip who preferred country life).

'The only way out was to be so good at school that the Head thought you were *brilliant* and went on so much about you that all your friends and relations began to refer to you as a "blue-stocking". And then, if you were ugly enough, you might just be allowed to attend Oxford University. And become something restful, like an archaeologist in Mesopotamia . . .

'I worked hard at being brilliant. And ugly.

'It was amazing how ugly you could make yourself in those days, if you kept your hair in greasy rats'-tails by applying Vaseline every night; and complained about your eyesight till your parents bought you spectacles. Then, unlike now, men did not make passes at girls who wore glasses.

'All this, Charlie the cat deeply appreciated, almost in a sinister way. When I burnt the midnight oil in study, he sat on my desk and kept me awake with his sharp anxious purring and beaming blue-eyed approval. He grew to be a connoisseur of the smell of Vaseline. He rubbed against my legs each morning, as I crushed my burgeoning bosom with the tightest possible undergarments, kept from my innocent childhood.

'But all to no avail. When I was seventeen, and the

satisfyingly great despair of my father, my glamorous aunt was summoned from Paris, and her eyes were the eyes of the haut monde. She pronounced me an undiscovered English rose; and the Vaseline in my hair didn't fool her either. Under her iron hand, I was transformed into a reluctant vision for my year of Coming Out. Fodder for the young men . . .

'Oh, it was a lovely year on the whole, Granddaughter, a whirl of soirées and dinners, music and glitter, champagne and driving home in the dawn. (All the brighter for the looming shadow of Hitler, for it was 1937 by that time.) The only part I hated was when the young men called hopefully at our house. At which point my father and mother, aunt et al. would traitorously desert me in the prettiest drawing room.

'Some of the young men I felt sorry for; victims, like myself, of duty and the great British mating game. Some, I hated. And a few I even rather liked.

'As I said, I was left alone.

'But never unprotected.

'No sooner had the door closed on my mother's saccharine blessings than Charlie would emerge from his favourite lurking-place, behind the long red velvet curtains.

'His technique was never the same with two young men running. Some, he simply sat and stared at, with his squinting and unnerving blue gaze. That disposed of those nervous of cats. Of course, they couldn't flee the room instantly, poor things. But sweating palms are the cure for love . . .

'With the bolder spirits, Charlie simply sat on the sofa between us, bent double, washing his less polite parts. If they still tried to press their advances, Charlie would begin to growl.

' "Is he . . . fierce?" they would ask.

' "Tigerish!" I would reply with glee.

'If growls were not enough, Charlie would simply make a vile smell. Cats can, you know, though they very seldom do, being polite creatures. Then the young man would wonder if I had made the smell; or whether I thought he had made the smell. Either way, it was an unfailing impediment . . .

'Charlie had a knack of sensing the nicer ones. He would suddenly grow passionate, stretching himself up the length of them, purring wildly and covering their immaculate suits with pale cat-hairs. The nicer ones eventually discovered they would rather stroke Charlie than stroke me, and usually ended up talking cheerfully about their own cats and dogs at home. When Charlie loved, he really loved; and he was a great flatterer . . .

'As for those few young men rendered desperate by lust for me, or a desire for my money . . . when a cat has been sick down your front, there is little you can do but call a taxi.

'Oh, I could have defended myself all right, if I'd had to; but only at the expense of hurt pride and bad feeling, which would have harmed my father's business. Charlie made it so easy, and his techniques were a joy to watch.

'So I finished my year of Coming Out heart-whole, donned my blue stockings and went to Oxford. At Oxford, Charlie became a total swell. Swaggered in his bejewelled black satin collar, subscribed to by all his admirers. Went to every party with me, learnt to walk down the High on a leash, got featured in *Isis* and nominated Party-cat of the Year for his ability to lap champagne yet still retain his perfect balance while leaping from bookcase to bookcase.

'And then Hitler spoilt it all.

'The winter of 1940–41 was dreadful in London. It wasn't just the Blitz. All our servants had gone to work in munitions, even Cook at her age. Charlie was bereft of those supporters who'd allowed him to roam the house at will. He was confined to the kitchen, now damp for lack of occupants. He developed a racking cough. He acquired a habit of being sick that was not deliberate. He could no longer control himself, and there was no one to nurse him. I was driving an ambulance by that time; my father was working on Economic Warfare all the hours God sent; and my mother was on so many committees for the War Effort that we hardly ever saw her.

'My father, who'd always loathed Charlie (and had strong suspicions about his sabotaging the efforts to make me a blushing bride), said Charlie had to go. There was no spare money to keep him in the vet's kennels either. He would have to be put down.

'I remember I was nursing Charlie on my knee at the time; in front of the fire, wrapped in a tartan rug, and he was still shivering. His coat, once so beautiful, was thin and yellow and staring; and his muscles, long as sleek as silk, were just gone. He felt all bones. It's *terrifying* how rapidly cats go downhill, once they get ill.

'I remember I looked at Charlie, and he looked up at me. That third eyelid was spreading across his dull eyes, but there was still a ghost of the old blue glint in them. I remembered how often he'd saved me in the past, warmed my loneliness, been the only one I could tell my feelings to.

'Then I looked at my father. However bad the rationing was, I thought, my father was not going short at his club. Whoever was going shabby and threadbare, my father still wore a good suit. And when had my father last listened to me, comforted me, been on *my* side?

'A little voice inside my head warned me to work out who my friends really were, before it was too late.

' "Do you remember when I was twelve, Daddy, and Charlie first came as a kitten? Do you remember what I said then?"

' "Of course I don't," he said, all bluff and bluster. "How the devil would I remember a thing like that?" But his hot dark eyes grew uneasy.

' "If Charlie goes, I go," I said.

' "You wouldn't last ten minutes on your own. What would you live on?"

'I knew my allowance was flying out of the window. But I just said:

' "I've got my pay as an ambulance driver."

' "You couldn't live on that!"

' "I know lots of girls who do!"

' "You'd better go and join them then. Come back when you've come to your senses."

' "I'll do just that."

'It was pride that got me through our front door. Pride and Charlie. I despaired of Charlie's life; but I was going to find him a place to die in peace. Preferably in my arms.

'Actually, it couldn't have been easier. The other girls

at the ambulance depot looked at me as I walked in, suitcase in one hand, Charlie in his basket in the other.

' "Been bombed out, love? Hard luck. Come and muck in with us. We can squeeze one more little one in."

'And, amazingly, they could. The one thing that wasn't in short supply in London was places to live, in spite of the bombing. Everybody who could leave London had. You could get a great big house, nearly as big as my home, for four quid a week, furnished. Pack it with eight cheerfully sloppy girl ambulance drivers and you had the merriest place in the world. What one of our boy-friends called a festival on a rubbish-tip.

'Charlie's reaction was amazing. With so many females to fuss over him, he simply got better, almost on the spot. Unless one of the girls slipped him some patent cure . . .

'It wasn't until the worst of that year's Blitz was over that the penny dropped.

'Charlie had got me away from home and my father for good. I still went for Sunday lunch, but even that was a bore and a burden, though I enjoyed the decent meal my mother laid on.

'I looked at Charlie across the room one night, as he lay stretched in the loving arms of a little blonde from Clerkenwell and I thought to myself:

' "What next, Charlie, what next?"

'And then we had the American invasion. A lot of my new friends simply seemed to lose their heads over the Americans. Our house floated in a sea of Spam and chewing-gum, nylons and Hershey bars.

'Myself, I was not impressed. They were so noisy, and wore tight trousers over fat bottoms . . . but there was one nice quiet captain in the Army Air Corps from Omaha. He wanted to become a professor of archaeology when he got demobbed, and we had some good chats about Mesopotamia . . .

'But Charlie was always on guard. It was not that he disliked the captain; he loved him almost too much. He was in his arms the moment he arrived, and he did not leave his arms till the captain departed. Which didn't hold up the talk about Mesopotamia, but it didn't leave room for anything else.

'Then my poor captain died over Germany; and I was relieved I had not loved him more. I think Charlie moped worse than I did. He took to peeing over every American uniform that came anywhere near me.

'Until one night there was a new American uniform in our common room, the room where we played the piano and the gramophone and danced, the room that had seen so much.

'The new American uniform wasn't tall, but very slim and wiry. Older than most of them, a little leathery, a little wrinkled. The crew-cut hair was greying. All the other uniforms had drawn back a little from him, in a respectful circle. The new uniform grinned a lopsided grin, as if he knew me. Said my name in a way that made my heart skip a beat oddly.

'Blue bright eyes twinkled at me, full of . . . not the usual American brashness, but a sort of lopsided fun, that filled the world with comic possibilities.

'Then the new uniform leaned across to one of the regular uniforms, who was playing the piano with a fag in the corner of his mouth, his eyes crinkled against the smoke, and his cap still on.

' "Soldier, do you always carry lethal weapons in your hat? It's a most unsafe practice . . . "

'A slender wiry hand tweaked the cap off, and revealed a hand-grenade inside. The hand took the grenade, pulled the pin out, and threw the grenade into the middle of the carpet.

'Everyone was screaming their heads off, before a large red flag emerged from the grenade, carrying the single word

'BANG!

' "Charlie," I said. "Charlie Ferber."

'He was Major Ferber by then. Thirty-nine years young, as he said. He'd tried to get on flying bombers, but the USAF told him they couldn't afford that many bombers, and had put him on entertaining the troops instead.

'Funny, but in spite of his greying hair he seemed younger than he had when I was twelve.

'And I still loved him. He made the world all right. He made the world an exciting place to be.

' "How's your father?" he asked with a wince.

' "Who's my father?" I said and laughed. I somehow knew he was going to ask me to marry him, and I somehow knew I was going to say yes. The future stretched before us . . .

'It was then the bomb dropped. Or rather, bombs. One in the gardens at the back of the house, and one in the street in front. Not big bombs; just a sneak raider, for it was the spring of 1944 by then, and the Germans were only sending over single fighter-bombers.

'None of us was hurt. Our windows had been boarded up and sandbagged years before. Within a few moments, the party was in full swing again. Most of the houses round us were empty shells, anyway . . .

'But I suddenly said:

' "Charlie, where's Charlie?"

'The cat was nowhere to be seen. I went to the back door and yelled for him; then the front. No reply. No plaintive mew. I grew frantic.

' "I must go and search for him! He could be lying injured!"

' "He's gone, hon," said Charlie Ferber behind me in the doorway.

' "Gone, gone where?" I peered at him in the gloom of the front hall.

' "Gone where good old cats go," said Charlie Ferber. "He was gone *before* the bombs dropped, hon."

' "What do you *mean*?" I was very uneasy.

' "His job was done. He kept you safe, till I came back for you. Over all these years . . . "

'I searched for his blue eyes. But, in the dimness, they were no more than two points of light, red reflections of a small fire that had broken out in a long-bombed house across the road.

' "He left you this," said Charlie Ferber. And handed me the last old tattered satin collar, that Charlie the cat had worn till the end.

'I remembered what he was, and shivered. Remembered that "magician" has two meanings. One is the jovial laughing man walking on to the stage and taking off his white gloves and showing the audience he has nothing up his sleeve.

'And the other, lost in the depths of time . . . sorceror . . . wizard?

' "Charlie?"

' "Don't ask any more, hon. I wouldn't have told you this much, only you were worried about the cat."

'His voice was strangely . . . pleading.

' "But . . . the cat is all right . . . wherever his is?"

' "Quite happy. More than happy."

'And he took me in his arms, in that dim hallway. And though the red reflections of the fire still shone in his eyes, the feel of his lean muscular body was . . . oh, so *familiar*, somehow. Even though he'd never kissed me before; or even held my hand.

' "Welcome back, Charlie," I said.'

My grandmother stopped talking, and stared into the fire. After a while I said:

'So that's how he became my grandfather?'

'Yes, I married him, even though I knew he was dangerous; oh, how dangerous! A lot of men are dangerous, my dear. You'll find that out one day. But then a really harmless man isn't much of a challenge to a girl . . . and Charlie was dangerous in such an exciting way.'

'Didn't your father and mother mind?'

'We were married before they knew it. Charlie had turned up that night with a special licence in his pocket. Oh, the *certainty* of that man. And he went out of his way to be nice to my parents. But they were nervous of him till the day they died. Well, my father, anyway. My mother was more . . . fascinated. She'd always had a soft spot for Charlie Ferber.'

She looked at me sideways. 'So . . . if you see ghost

cats, you've no need to worry. It's only a little bit of Charlie Ferber coming out in you; though you never knew him.'

'I can't think of anything nicer,' I said.

And meant it.

Henry Marlborough

Zillah Salisbury, getting out of the white Rolls. Walking up the church path, on her father's arm.

Beyond the blackened tombstones, a clutter of women had gathered, clutching children and prams and flowery headscarves against the cold March wind. Three separate notes in the sound of their voices. Wonder at the beauty of her dress. A sort of dreadful avid cooing. And a third voice, one rough woman's voice calling:

'Best of luck, love!'

That voice caught in Zillah's mind like a fish-hook. Not an unkind voice, but full of old pain. Hoping against hope for her happiness, and hoping in vain.

Zillah nearly screamed; how could that woman know what was in her mind?

The church path was long; old tombstones laid end to end. Beautiful curling, whirling lettering on the damp near-black stone, under the toes of her white satin shoes as they came and went under the lifted hem of her dress.

'Head *up*,' hissed her father. 'You're not going to a bloody funeral!'

Zillah nearly screamed again. First the rough-voiced woman, now her father. She'd tried to build a shell of cheerfulness round her misery. Was even *that* a failure?

Did they all know she didn't want to get married? That she wished it *was* her funeral?

Nobody pried into the dead; they even averted their eyes from the coffin. The dead had privacy, and the power to frighten.

Brides were decorated sacrificial victims, into whom every eye could pry, every sly voice poke. The jokes Uncle Walter would make at the wedding breakfast; the witty asides of Geoffrey's friends. Stale jokes that never lost their sting, lying in ambush for her slightest blush. Jokes brought from Geoffrey's stag-party, along with the hangovers.

Everybody had a piece of the bride; nobody dared rape the dead.

'Head UP,' hissed her father. She lifted it, and stared at the pitiless blue sky; at the old wooden trees, leafless, without a point of green. Last season's leaves lay on the tombstones of the path, crackling underfoot, like the sere brown ghosts of other possible lives she'd left behind at the church gate. Dreams of going to London, having her own flat, working abroad. Being *somebody*.

At one point, the leaves had gathered like a strike-picket, six inches deep, right across the path. As if they wanted to stop her getting into the church, turn her back towards the infinite possibilities.

'C'mon,' her father urged her forward, as if he was ready to pull her along by main force. 'We're late.'

She stepped among the heaped-up leaves, in her low frail shoes. Immediately a big leaf worked down inside her shoe, spiking her soft instep like a nail. She limped on three steps, but the pain was quite unbearable. She pulled her arm out of her father's, stooped, and saw, carved on the tombstone, the name:

HENRY MARLBOROUGH, WIDOWER

There were dates, other writing, but she hadn't time to read them. Her father was tugging at her, hissing that she was making a spectacle of him, in front of the whole town.

She pulled the leaf-spike from her shoe, and read one more line of lettering.

HE BUILDED HYS HOUS ON SAND

What a cruel thing to put on anybody's tombstone. What had he done to deserve that?

Her father yanked her away. She passed into the dark doorway, and did all that was required of her, without fault, so that they praised her for it, afterwards. But she remembered neither the declaration nor the vow. They remained a blank for ever after. She spent the time, and the miseries of the wedding breakfast afterwards, anaesthetised by wondering who Henry Marlborough had been, and why he had builded his house on sand. She felt a sympathy. Now it was too late, she knew it was exactly what she was doing herself.

She should never have said yes to Geoffrey Williams. She knew that now. But he'd been so *comfortable*. Infant playmate, childhood sweetheart. And by the time she'd come down from university, all her other old boy-friends had gone: to practise town planning in Exeter, or work for the National Trust in the Lake District. Only Geoffrey remained, an ex-student like herself, comfortingly clinging to his college scarf and old sports car. There was only Geoffrey to talk radical politics with, only Geoffrey who would take her to watch Shakespeare in Bradford and listen to Mozart in Leeds. Nobody thought anything of Mozart in Smilesby; he'd written nothing for brass bands . . .

And Geoffrey had never been sexually pushy. Holding hands, cuddles in the car, a kiss on the doorstep were enough to keep him happy. Which suited her.

Above all, she could talk to him about the great big world outside Smilesby; talk about escape from their all-devouring families. He listened in sympathetic silence to her tirades against her father; made faint rebellious murmurs about his own; told her that as a chartered surveyor he could make a living anywhere.

She'd believed, given time, she could lick Geoffrey into shape; and then they could plan their escape together. So when he proposed to her for the fourth time, she said yes to him, and they fixed the date.

And then the trap slammed shut on her. His parents were delighted. Her parents were delighted. His father made him a partner in the firm. Her father (who had never taken the slightest interest in Geoffrey before) suddenly began slapping him on the back, leading him away for a quiet chat and a whisky, and introducing him to all and sundry as '*my* future son-in-law'. It was not she who was starting to lick Geoffrey into shape; it was her father. A total takeover bid; and Geoffrey was loving every moment of it.

The last time she and Geoffrey had dinner alone before the wedding, she tried to put her foot down. He must promise to get a job as far away from Smilesby as possible, as soon as possible.

He looked at her as if she was mad. 'And give up my

partnership? Thirty thousand a year? To go and work for a slave-driving stranger? Be *reasonable*, Zillah. I know you don't want to live on top of your father. We could go and live at Broughley if you like . . . '

He said that as a great concession. Broughley was ten miles away. A ten-minute run in her father's Jag. Practically next door . . .

She nearly broke it off then. But she hadn't the courage. Not two days before the wedding, with a wedding breakfast for four hundred guests, and all the presents arriving, and everybody who was anybody in the county coming. She couldn't do that to him. Not looking at his gentle, sheepish, reasonable face . . .

Not in the face of her father's intolerable wrath . . .

They set up home in a rented furnished house. It wasn't Geoffrey's fault; the money was there. Geoffrey and his family were stinking rich. They had been to look over many houses for sale before the wedding. But Zillah always ended up saying it wasn't worth buying when they weren't staying long. Now Geoffrey tried to buy a house again. But she found them all intolerable because Geoffrey approved of them, which meant that his father and her father would approve of them. She imagined Geoffrey's parents coming to dinner, Geoffrey's friends coming round for a drink and a game of Trivial Pursuit. That was enough. She found fault with all the houses, tore them to pieces with a decisive viciousness that surprised even herself. She had seldom been vicious in her life, and never decisive. Now, although she still didn't know what she wanted, she knew with appalling rage what she didn't want.

Of course, family and friends came to the rented house. But that didn't matter, because there was nothing of *her* in it. It was a huge new four-bedroomed detached, with quarrelling rooflines. Its only claim to uniqueness was a round window in the downstairs toilet. It was built of bricks that looked like Lego. All the houses looked as if they'd been built of Lego, by a child with no gift for it. The house lay in a dog-legged cul-de-sac, at the end of a lot of wildly intersecting roads of similar houses. The old village with its church lay a mile away. This was Nowhere. Only the view of a distant ridge of hills, seen through the picture-window of the dining room, was real.

One evening, under the cover of dinner with his parents, Geoffrey plucked up courage to say they'd settled down very comfortably, and the house was handy for town. He might well make the owner an offer for it . . .

A kind of tiger broke loose inside Zillah; a tiger of mad black rage. She had only enough energy to *contain* the tiger so it didn't leap out and destroy the other three people sitting round the table. All she could do otherwise was to sit and glare at Geoffrey in silence.

The silence went on and on. The others sensed the tiger, even though they couldn't see it. They began to twitch, look down at the tablecloth, fiddle with their napkins and roll the half-eaten bread on their sideplates into little grey balls. Mama and Papa each tried to start a change of topic, ran over each other, and collapsed back into silence. Finally Geoffrey, white as a sheet, asked Zillah if she was feeling unwell?

She took the chance; ground out something about a blinding headache, and was excused. Fled to the bedroom and listened to the rumble of their voices downstairs. Hesitant, baffled. Not at all the usual way they talked.

She thought with sad satisfaction that they were beginning to grasp that the marriage was a mistake.

Next morning, she realised that Geoffrey had become scared of her.

She had been permitted to go on working for her father, until they started a family. The work remained as boring as ever. She was no more than a glorified legal secretary and the boss's daughter.

Of course she had her degree in English, got by commuting daily to York University. But to her father, it had always been just that: of-course-a-degree-in-English. Something to keep her occupied, till she got married. A sensible alternative to an expensive foreign finishing-school. Something to boast about to his friends. After she got her degree and didn't know what to do with it, her father suggested secretarial training; with increasing force. It was the line of least resistance. It avoided having her father shouting at her. After that, not knowing who she wanted to work for, and not quite inclined to leave home and set up in a strange town, she had drifted into the family firm.

Now, she felt a stranger everywhere. At the firm, at home, at her parents' home. One lunch-hour she was drifting around the town, feeling lost and looking at things she didn't want to buy, when she happened to pass the churchyard.

By now, the leaves were out, the new grass an intoxicating green, and the churchyard *invited.* She passed between the gate-columns, with their blackened classical urns, and felt instantly at home, at rest. She felt none of the bad things in her life had ever really happened. She felt new-born; *right*. She heard the birds singing for the first time in weeks. Since the wedding, in fact.

She remembered Henry Marlborough, who had builded his house on sand, and walked up the path slowly, looking for his tombstone. Crouched to read it, one long slender finger tracing the whirling, curling words.

HENRY MARLBOROUGH, WIDOWER
AND BREWER. BORN 1632 OBIT
TWELFTH DAIE OF IANUARY IN THE YEERE
OF OUR LORD 1722
BEING WIDOED AT AN EARLY AGE HEE
RAISED HYS FIVE CHILDREN
IN THE FEERE OF GOD AND IN KINDNESSE
LIVING IN HOPE
OF ANOTHER WYFE
HEE BUILDED A NEW HOUS THAT SHEE
MIGHT COME TO IT
BUT SHEE CAME NOT
HE BUILDED HYS HOUS ON SAND

Poor Henry Marlborough! He sounded nice, raising his children in kindness. An old man sitting in his new house, waiting, waiting in vain. Dying, still waiting. *Poor* Henry Marlborough!

She sat down on the table-tomb next door and wept for him and for herself. Harder and longer than she would have thought possible. She was terrified somebody might come and make a fuss. But nobody came and finally her tears ceased of their own accord. She dried her face on her too-small handkerchief, made what repairs to her make-up she could, decided she looked a wreck in the small round mirror and went back to work oddly comforted.

After that, she took her lunch to the churchyard every fine day. It wasn't gloomy, like the Victorian churchyard across the road. The tombstones were old, ivy-covered. The newest was a little marble urn to Laetitia Powell, who had died aged but half her age, in the year of Trafalgar. She grew fond of Laetitia, and others. For the stones carried not just names, but occupations. Tanner, blacksmith, carpenter. A whole Georgian town, busy hands at last laid to rest. But friends; a family. And the place was full of birds, who came for crumbs. And a sly tabby cat who came to catch birds, but settled amicably and delicately for a paste sandwich on the tombtop instead.

She assured herself she was not being *morbid*. On Fridays, she brought the local paper to read, sitting on the table-tomb with her feet stretched out companionably to Henry Marlborough; browsing through such safe unemotional items as the price of larch-lap fencing.

That was how she saw the notice of the sale. A house-clearance at Dyke Bank Farm. She'd been to Dyke Bank once with Grandpa, when she was little. She remembered the grey stone house tucked into the fold of a hill, low and dark. Suddenly she wanted to go. She wanted some lowness and darkness, after the house she had to live in. She'd never been to a sale. Next Wednesday afternoon, her half-day! She'd go. A sudden tiny shaft of excitement shot through her, like a sunbeam, like a new-sprouting blade of grass. She had the delightful illusion she was starting to grow again.

She wished to God she hadn't mentioned the sale to Father; she did so only to ensure he wouldn't keep her late on Wednesday with extra typing. Father told Geoffrey at the weekend dinner-party of course, and Geoffrey not only insisted on coming but on taking the whole thing over. Poking round the low dark rooms, rubbishing everything. The instant antiques expert.

She wished he'd drop down dead. Those stupid, *stupid* questions about was it Chippendale, when anybody could see it wasn't that sort of stuff. It was *country* stuff, old, clumsily repaired a hundred years ago, dirty, greasy and *real*. Spindle-back armchairs old men must have sat in for half a lifetime. A cupboard whose bottom drawer must have seen the birth of generations of kittens.

'Rubbish! Wouldn't give it house-room,' Geoffrey announced at last. 'C'mon, we've got better things to do on a sunny afternoon . . . '

'Like what?' asked Zillah dangerously. 'Squash? Having a gin-and-tonic with the chaps?'

He sensed the tiger loose inside her again, and backed off, nervously tapping his catalogue against his well-tailored thigh, waiting for the auctioneer to begin.

When the auctioneer did, Zillah found it terrifying. She raised her catalogue timidly, bidding for one or two of the chairs she liked, only to be swept aside by a flood of bids from scruffy men in greasy padded waistcoats who lounged across the larger bits of furniture at the back of the room. She lost three more chairs, before she could get her breath and courage back. The prices! One hundred, two hundred pounds. For one chair!

'So much for your *rubbish*,' she hissed at Geoffrey.

'They're bloody mad. You could get a Bang and Olufsen CD player for that!'

And then an old wooden rocker was held up. She thought it looked the kind of rocker Henry Marlborough might have sat in. She knew she had to have it. Again the bidding leapt away like a bolting horse. Two hundred. Two twenty-five. But she clung on like a terrified rider. Knowing she must not be beaten. For the sake of her life. She felt Geoffrey's restraining hand on her arm, and shook it off. She felt like burying her teeth in it.

'You must be bonkers,' Geoffrey said feebly.

'Oh, shut UP.'

The bidding paused. People began to stare at them, even the auctioneer. Geoffrey got to his feet and stalked out. She was delighted to see him go.

'The bidding is against you, madam,' said the auctioneer.

She consigned all her bank balance to perdition; all her childhood savings certificates; all her Telecom shares. Her determination must have shown in her voice. The other bidders fell away.

'Your bid has it, madam,' said the auctioneer wryly. 'No need to bid against yourself.'

There was a sympathetic titter around the room, and the chair was knocked down to her for three hundred pounds.

She would buy no more; she had frightened even herself. But she would stay until the end, savouring her victory and her freedom.

Which she did, feeling all glorious, fizzy, sweaty, flat and rejoicing. Until a certain dark old chest was held up by two porters.

'A marriage-chest of about 1690. Nicely carved. One bottom drawer. Touch of woodworm in the legs. Emblazoned with the initials HM:ZS. ZS is unusual, I must say. Can't be Zebediah, because it's on the wife's side.'

A little laughter, and a flood of bids.

ZS. Her own initials. She had to have it. And again that tone of utter determination, which all professional dealers learn to recognise and fear, came back into her voice.

She got it for four hundred. A quarter of all the money she had in the world.

It wasn't until she was gloating over it that it came to her that the other initials were HM.

She shivered from head to foot; but in a rather pleasant sort of way. She trembled so much she could hardly sign the cheque for the auctioneer's clerk.

The day the things were delivered, she spent the whole evening moving them from room to room. It was as well that Geoffrey had gone off to play squash. For even she had to admit they didn't fit anywhere. They fought savagely with the fiddly mahogany of the German fitted kitchen; exchanged insults with the leather sofas in the lounge. Made the repro Regency dining suite look like the tacky rubbish it was.

She began to feel desperate, like a child who has

brought home an unwanted kitten and knows her father will be angry. She felt *responsible* for the chair and chest. She had dragged them from their proper place, and made them lost and homeless. She was frightened that at any moment Geoffrey would appear and make her put them down in the thin tacky garden shed, where they would moulder away for ever.

Then she remembered the boxroom, that they never used or thought about. She flogged upstairs, grunting under the awkward weight of the chair. Opened the boxroom door with one hand, still clutching the chair with the other.

The boxroom greeted her.

Lying in bed that night, trying to be sensible, trying to think like a trained graduate, she attempted to work out just how the boxroom had 'greeted' her.

The boxroom was where all the sins of the builder had come home to roost. Not so much a boxroom as the bit left over; ridiculously long and narrow, with a sloping ceiling and a tiny window jammed into the far end, just to let in a bit of light.

It was the sloping ceiling and the little window. Just like her old bedroom at Grandpa's. And the sunset streaming in the tiny window, sending distorted bars of red light across the long wall. Like the sunsets at Grandpa's, when she lay in bed after a long lovely day with the dogs and chickens and calves, waiting to fall asleep. That was all . . .

But she knew deep down that hadn't been all. The red light on the long wall had been enchanted. She had felt that at any moment her dull grey prison of a world might crack and *anything* might happen.

She had dragged in the rocking-chair and sat and rocked, gently, dreamily, her eyes nearly shut. Reaching out to a presence that she *knew* was in the room with her. It was male but gentle. Middle-aged, easy-going. What's the fret, it seemed to say, what's the hassle? Take it steady!

She had sat and rocked a long time; till the long red bars of light finally faded to grey, and the room was empty again.

She didn't know what the presence in the room was, but she knew she wanted it more than anything in the world. She had got up and worked like a thing demented. Dragged everything else out of the room. There were only a few empty suitcases and Geoffrey's ridiculous exercise bicycle, which he had lost interest in even before they got married. *That* could go down in the garden shed!

She had stuffed the suitcases under beds, into the cupboard under the stairs. She had somehow got the chest upstairs, step by painful step, every muscle in her body screeching, sweaty hair flogging in her eyes. She had dragged it into the boxroom and sat again rocking, feeling the blurred carving of the initials that said HM:ZS. But the room had only been dark and empty.

She turned the key in the lock as she left; and hid it in her underwear drawer, as excited as an adulteress . . .

Still baffled at herself, she listened to Geoffrey's snores, turned over, and slept.

Geoffrey didn't notice about the boxroom. There was no reason why he should, until their next holiday.

They had more rooms than they knew what to do with.

Meanwhile, she did a lot by stealth. Got the ancient clippie rug that Grandpa had given her, from her old bedroom at home. Went to other farmhouse sales and found a small dark oak table and an upright ladderback chair. Paid far too much for a framed child's sampler, dated 1703, because just possibly Henry Marlborough might once have clapped eyes on it. She knew she had been a fool, but she didn't care. For the presence had come back, several times, as she sat rocking in the boxroom, and the sunset rays made their elongated patterns on the wall. She had smelt a smell, an old cobwebby farmhouse smell, when she closed her eyes. Her sensible self told her it was just the rug. But every time she felt lost or lonely now, she had only to think of her room, and she was comforted.

HM:ZS.

Was it only dead Grandpa or really Henry Marlborough? She imagined them being much alike. Middle-aged, grizzle-haired, sturdy, a little bow-legged from working with horses. Calm and wise. In the calm that the presence brought, she could think without pain of all the things that had happened to her.

Little things, like the sale when she'd bought the chair and chest. How scared she'd been. How her heart had thumped . . .

But how brave, said the presence in the room. You hung on, and hanging on when you feel scared *is* being brave. She began putting her feelings into words, telling the presence about it.

Tell the world, said the presence. The world is full of people too scared to . . .

Suddenly, something made her get up and run downstairs and fetch her portable typewriter. Put it on the little table by the window, sit in the ladderback chair and begin to type.

An hour later, she sat back finished. Looked out at the ridge of hills that must have changed so little since Henry Marlborough looked at them. Dazzled her eyes with what was left of the sunset. Then re-read the thing she had written.

It was quite good. Good enough for the local paper, anyway. Most of that was rubbish! It might give something to the readers; give humble people the courage to go and bid at auction themselves. She would send it. With a covering letter to the editor. She wrote the letter quickly, before her courage ran out. But when she came to sign it, she hesitated. She didn't dare sign her own name. She was too well-known in the town. Somebody would tell Geoffrey and her father . . .

So instead, she signed it 'Henry Marlborough'. Shoved it into an envelope and into her handbag, as Geoffrey barged in downstairs, yelling he'd brought two friends for supper.

The article was published the following week, on the entertainments page. She read it through three times, sitting on the table-tomb and swinging her legs. She still found it an interesting read, even with two misprints. The sun shone, the birds sang, and Henry Marlborough seemed to approve.

Two days later, a letter came from the editor. Addressed to Henry Marlborough of course. It said the editor would welcome further articles. And then a blue cheque fell out of the envelope. For fifteen pounds. Also made out to Henry Marlborough.

She stood on the doormat in her dressing-gown, filled with a sort of glory. Then Geoffrey clumped downstairs, blindly demanding if breakfast was ready? She had plenty of time to conceal letter and cheque in her dressing-gown pocket.

But over the day, her joy turned to fret. She was living a lie, and now there was money involved. She wanted to go on writing, and liked getting money for it. But now she would need a false bank account before she could cash the cheques. Telling lies about money was a crime. The police . . .

Once home, she fled to the sanctuary of the boxroom.

'What shall I do?'

She smelt the old smell; felt the atmosphere of middle-aged easy-going reasonableness. There was a fly buzzing at the little window, as frantic as herself. She reached over and opened the window and it flew out to freedom. So easy, when you're helped by somebody who knows the ropes!

See the editor and have it out with him.

As easy as that.

It wasn't easy at all. Making the appointment was easy, though the editor shouted down the phone so hard it hurt her ear. She learnt to hold the earpiece a couple of inches away, whenever she spoke to Miles Trumby, after that.

When she went to see him, she found out why he shouted. He sat in the centre of a large upstairs room, surrounded by his five minions who were all busy clacking away on hideously ancient typewriters, or yelling down the several phones which never seemed to stop ringing.

She had quite a lot of trouble making him understand that *she* was Henry Marlborough.

'But you're Councillor Salisbury's daughter,' he yelled, so that everybody heard. 'Mind you, I'm delighted to have Councillor Salisbury's daughter writing for my paper . . . '

She had a terrible ten minutes, explaining in a high-pitched scream that she didn't want to write as Councillor Salisbury's daughter. Her father wouldn't like it; her husband wouldn't like it. She wanted to make her own way. Her father must never know. The other reporters began to turn and give her curious glances, their ears visibly flapping. It would be all round the town now. She was close to tears. It had all gone so *wrong*.

Then Miles Trumby leant the bare skin of his elbows on the hard edge of the typewriter (she saw with horror that he had deep grooves in his elbows, worn in by years of leaning on that machine) and winked and said:

'What the old bugger doesn't know won't hurt him.' He called the room to some sort of silence. 'This, lads,' he said with a wink, 'is Henry Marlborough.'

'Hi, Henry,' said all the reporters with wide grins. She knew she was in; safe.

When she got home, she went straight to the box-room and rocked. Calmed down; stopped shivering with shock. The sweat cooled on her.

The room seemed to be saying that her latest crisis was over, and she had won. The room seemed to say that all life, afterwards, was a very little thing, though precious. But nothing, set against the ages that had been.

'It's all right for *you*,' she said. 'You're dead. For you, it doesn't hurt any more.'

She felt the room was amused.

The ideas for articles just seemed to float into her head, as she sat in the boxroom watching the ridge of hills, on the sunny evenings when Geoffrey was late home. One article was about a Georgian coaching inn, threatened with demolition after serving the town for nearly three hundred years. Another was about a newly opened stately home she'd just visited. A third was about an exhibition of early English map-makers, like Speed, at the local library.

They were all about things that Henry Marlborough would have understood.

After a month, Miles Trumby invited her to do a weekly column. People were interested; they were asking who Henry Marlborough was. He had just told them it was somebody in business in the town, who wanted to remain anonymous. They had all assumed it was a man, of course. That tickled Miles Trumby's fancy; she knew she had an ally for life, there.

So she set off on her weekly column. It made her care more and more deeply about the pretty old town. The town she shared with Henry Marlborough; just separated in time. The town she was looking after for Henry Marlborough. As the weeks passed, she learnt more and more about Smilesby, with its Yorkshire pantiled roofs, and grey stone walls.

Present-day Smilesby she learnt about from Miles

and his cynical pack; the dirt about everything and everybody. She got into the habit of dropping in after work every Monday evening, with her piece. Miles always held up her beautiful typing as an example to what he called, 'These scruffy young tykes. They still type with one finger and I've even got to spell their four-letter words for them.'

She would be offered tea in a very stained mug, and accepted with alacrity. It was part of her initiation; it made her a reporter. They helped her fill in her application form to join the NUJ. She became their mascot. They fed her more and more dubious stories, calling to each other that each one was 'a bit thick – not fit for ladies' ears'. Sometimes they offered to take her for a drink after work. But she drew the line there. Small towns had eyes and ears . . .

But it was Old Smilesby that was her love. The parish church, once the scene of her torment, became a fount of knowledge. Henry Marlborough must have worshipped there every Sunday, sitting in a box-pew with his five children, till he was an old, old man. Still watching, during the long long sermons, for the wife who was to come.

The walls were thick with memorial tablets. She read every one, noting the dates carefully.

'Noden Slater, notable physician 1657–1725' might have attended Henry on his despairing deathbed.

'Spencer Norris, taylour, 1669–1740' might have made him greatcoats in earlier times.

At the public library, she learned that Brooke Street was the first Georgian terrace to be built in Smilesby. Henry Marlborough must have often walked down it in the rain, and run for shelter under the arches of the Butter Cross. She learned with awe that the fields and hedges round Smilesby were Georgian fields and hedges. There was a huge oak on the Wretby road, where Henry Marlborough might have drawn in his horse for a breather in the shade, on his way home from market.

Every spare moment she read old books, or prowled the town looking for Georgian objects; the milestone in Cater Street, the sandstone mounting-block in front of the King's Head.

Henry Marlborough was in full cry.

It happened on one of the Saturday nights she dreaded. Once a month, her parents and Geoffrey's came for dinner. Oh, she was a good enough cook. They praised her for it, looked forward to her meals with rather gluttonous gusto. Meals she hardly touched herself, because she felt they choked her. If she'd eaten more than two mouthfuls, she knew she'd have thrown up.

These four were the architects of her prison. They had planned her marriage to Geoffrey between them. From the first time Geoffrey had asked her out to a concert at Thirsk, they had planned it. A marriage of commerce. The firm of Williams and Mickleton, the county's leading estate agents, had had a lot to offer Tripps, Salisbury and Tripps, Solicitors and Commissioners for Oaths.

So she sat now and listened to them talking, and hated them. They ignored her as usual, once they had praised her cooking. They were talking about the houses in Brooke Street. (At least the men were. Her mother and Mrs Williams were wittering on as usual about the rudeness of modern shop-assistants.)

She heard her father say:

'You've got them, then?'

'Number eleven to number twenty-seven. He was glad to sell. They're not in good nick.'

'They've got planning protection. They're listed buildings.'

'Knock a few tiles off, and let the rain in. Dry rot'll do the rest. Once they're condemned, in we go with the supermarket. Chief Planner won't make any trouble. He owes me a favour for Brydon Road.'

They were talking about Brooke Street. Down which Henry Marlborough had once walked.

She watched Brooke Street for the next month. Noted the beginnings of decay. Empty houses; broken panes in beautiful sash windows; long dead grass in the gardens, behind the elegant rusting railings. Nobody cared about Brooke Street. It was in the town centre and the houses were small and damp. Only pensioners lived there now.

At the end of the month, she saw workmen on the roof of number twenty. Not repairing it. Breaking tiles with hammers and sending down showers of fragments into the weedy garden. Laughing.

She went home nearly in tears. Geoffrey would not be home till eight. She went into the boxroom and rocked and rocked.

The smell came. And the calmness. It was enough. She sat down at her little table and put a sheet of paper in her typewriter.

Fury and hate surged through her fingers. Five sheets of typescript boiled from the machine. She didn't even bother to read it over, just stuffed it into an envelope, took it to the end of the road and posted it.

Miles looked at her across his littered inky desk and shook his head sadly.

'It's no good then?' she asked, crushed.

'Oh, it's *good*. Best thing you've done. Only . . . this newspaper has got to live with people in the town . . . afterwards. We can't afford a libel action. You don't like your father-in-law, do you? Or your father, much?'

'I hate them.'

Miles pursed his lips and looked worried.

'So you won't use it?' she shouted. 'You're scared of them! You don't care!' She was in a fury with Miles too now.

'Oh, I can *use* it,' said Miles. 'In my own way. There's more ways than one of skinning a cat.'

'Like *what*?'

'Wait and see. Only I think we'd better leave Henry Marlborough out of it, eh?'

She watched it grow from tiny beginnings, into a storm.

First a letter about the workmen breaking tiles, signed 'Worried Pensioner, Brooke Street'.

Then an indignant editorial from Miles, about taking care of Our Smilesby Heritage.

Then a letter from a Labour councillor, asking who actually *owned* Brooke Street.

Then a letter from a lecturer in architecture at York University, underlining Brooke Street's historical importance.

Then a letter from the Georgian Society.

Then an article in the national *Guardian* headlined 'The Rape of Smilesby'. Then an answering one in the *Telegraph* questioning the strength of the planning laws.

The local MP took up the cause . . .

Mr Williams and her father, at the monthly dinner-party, cursing with sudden obscene rage about the planning committee and interfering southerners and their blasted unusable row of houses.

'Satisfied?' asked Miles, the next time she saw him.

'Very,' she said, with savage joy. 'All these people writing articles . . . '

'Mainly me and the lads,' said Miles. 'The national papers paid us very well. And Tom here made a marvellous "Worried Pensioner".'

Amid raucous laughs from the pack, Miles pushed three letters forward. 'These are for you. County magazine wants three thousand words on "The Heritage of Smilesby". They're offering seventy-five quid. And the *Guardian* and the *Telegraph* want follow-ups. They pay well an' all. Does Henry Marlborough fancy having a crack at it?'

'But Miles, they've asked *you* to do it!'

'You've earned your share of the loot. I'll help you lick your articles into shape.'

'Oh, *Miles*!'

She left his office walking on air.

Her father never found out who'd blown the whistle on Brooke Street. Trouble came from a different direction. As they were packing for their winter skiing holiday, Geoffrey found the boxroom locked and demanded the key.

'It's all my things in there!' she flared. 'It's private.'

'What do you mean, *private*? It's my house – I pay the rent!'

She knew there'd be no stopping him now. She fetched the key and flung the door open herself.

Things had moved on a bit. There was an eighteenth-century grandfather clock, by a Smilesby maker, that she'd never dared to wind, for fear of Geoffrey hearing its tick. There was a crude dim oil painting of a middle-aged man in floppy white shirt and leather waistcoat, that she dreamed one day might turn out to be Henry himself. Both bought with her journalism earnings at Wednesday sales. And there were heaps of scribbled-over typescript on her desk.

'Christ,' said Geoffrey. 'What's this – a junk-shop?'

'My room,' she said slowly, letting the tiger start to prowl and letting Geoffrey see her face. 'My *study*, where I write. You can have the rest of the house, to do what you like with. But this is mine. I'll pay you rent for it. Now get out.'

His mouth opened and closed silently, as if he was some pale pink fish. Then he got out.

She stayed to wind the clock for the first time, before she locked the room again and followed him downstairs. They ate their meal in ominous silence. Then he got up and left the house in a hurry.

She just knew he had gone to consult the gang of four.

Stupidly, they saved up their ambush for the monthly dinner-party. Guessing it was coming, she served curry.

Not the mild sweet curry that her mother-in-law simpered over, but a real scorcher that must have taken the skin off their mouths.

'Like the curry, mother-in-law? It's a new recipe . . .'

Mother-in-law nodded mutely, tears starting to roll down her cheeks from the taste.

That should have warned them; but they were so used to winning.

Her father went plunging in. Time you two settled down. Started a family. About time Zillah made them grandparents . . . all his friends at the Conservative Club were grandfathers now . . . The fault lay in young wives being allowed to go on working . . . he was giving her a month's notice! The awful thing was that it was said with such waggish joviality. As if it were all some splendid joke.

'Are you giving me the sack, Father?'

The edge in her voice, so inappropriate, so inhospitable, half-warned him. He was amazed that she was turning one of his little jokes into a public row.

'Don't take it to heart, m'dear. It's for your own good!'

'I shall just have to find another job then, shan't I?'

'Who'd give *you* a job?'

That stung her. 'Why not? After all, I am a trained legal secretary.'

A dreadful look crept over her father's face. 'Who's made you an offer? That old bastard Smurthwaite?'

Smurthwaite and Smurthwaite were the only other firm of solicitors in Smilesby.

It was not in her nature to tell lies. But

she didn't have to. In his panic, he beat himself.

'What'll the town say, if they hear you've gone from me to them?'

She just smiled sweetly.

'How much is he offering you?'

'You could try raising my salary, Father. I might consider staying.'

'You wouldn't do *that* to me . . . your own father? You wouldn't *go*?'

'I damn well would.' She was amazed she could talk to her father like that. But the gossip round the newspaper office had cut him down to size. He was no longer the terrible tyrant king of her childhood. Just a fat ageing man, with broken veins in his cheeks. Old Geordie Salisbury, who got his fingers burnt with Brooke Street.

He glared at her. She glared right back, letting the tiger loose a bit. He dropped his eyes first.

'How much d'you want?'

'Try an extra thousand.'

'Five hundred.' He didn't part with his money easy, did old Geordie Salisbury; Miles always said so.

'A thousand. And the old records room as my office. I'm sick of sitting with your typists.'

'That I should have lived to see the day . . . ' He seemed dazed.

She struck while the iron was hot. 'Do I get it, or don't I?'

'Oh, aye . . . I *hate* talking money round a meal-table.'

She almost said, 'You didn't mind talking about Brooke Street!' But she bit her tongue in time.

Her victory left her trembling. She was shocked he'd given in so easily. Suddenly, he looked old, beaten. It left a gap in her life. She was glad, when they'd all gone home, to sit and rock for a few minutes in the peaceful dark of the boxroom.

She took Henry Marlborough to the office with her; or rather the man in the oil painting, with his floppy white shirt and leather waistcoat. She took the grandfather clock, too. It impressed the clients, like a real lawyer's clock should.

The old records office was Dickensian; her father had shoved all his old furniture in there, when he went over to modern Danish teak. She polished the old furniture; and the blackened brass push-bell, till it shone like gold. Used it to summon a typist when she needed one. She went on going to the house sales; acquired a tithe-map of Smilesby parish; acquired an old warming-pan with initials punched into the lid. The initials were very worn; but they could've been HM as much as anything else.

On fine days, that following spring, she still went to the churchyard. On wet days she stayed in her office and talked to the portrait, planning her articles and dreaming her dreams. She now had three places in the world that seemed real to her. Four if you counted the auctions.

'I want to talk to you,' said Geoffrey, fiddling with his knife and fork.

'Go on, then. I won't charge you a consultation fee.' She watched him flinch, with some satisfaction. What a weed he seemed now! Still, a harmless weed who paid the bills and let her save her own salary towards . . . what? Freedom?

A weed who was hardly ever at home. He went to his mother's, the country club, squash. Anywhere but home. Convenient, really.

'My mother and father keep nagging me,' he said, petulantly. 'They think we ought to have a kid. After all, you're nearly twenty-seven . . . '

'Past my breeding peak, you mean?'

'Oh, leave off, will you? I'm *serious*.'

She considered. A baby might have its advantages. She was tired of working in her father's office, in spite of her new status. There was no future in being a legal secretary, soothing down clients with trays of tea. If she was at home all day, she'd have more time to write . . .

On the other hand, they hadn't made love for six months now, and that was the way she liked it. On the honeymoon, for all his sexual innuendoes, Geoffrey had come at her with all the sensitivity and subtlety of the Charge of the Light Brigade. With equally disastrous results.

Since then . . . she remembered a hooked fish twisting and coiling on the river bank, and the stray dog passing that had been fascinated by it, and yet at the same time terrified of picking it up. Poking at it, then retreating. She and Geoffrey had become like that fish and dog.

Yet she looked at him now, not with any sort of love, but with a twist of compassion. He wasn't any sort of monster, just a prisoner of life, like herself. She would like to help get his bullying parents off his back.

And she had this vision of a dark cool old house,

and the child asleep in its pram, in the sunshine, outside the French window, and herself busy writing . . .

'OK,' she said. 'We'll look for a house. If we find one I like, I'll give your parents their grandchild.'

Next day, panic set in. With a child, she'd be helpless. Two sets of grandparents would just roll all over her, like steamrollers. With a child, she'd be their prisoner forever. You couldn't run away to London to be a writer, once you had a child; no matter how many possible contacts you had in Fleet Street.

But she had a way out. If she didn't like any of the houses she saw, she didn't *have* to have a child.

The next four weeks saw a massacre of house-agents. Her tongue excelled itself in sharpness.

'A flat-roofed 1930s monstrosity!'

'What do we want a swimming pool *for*? They just fill up with dead leaves.'

'Just like Southfork with pantiles!'

Most house-agents writhed silently, and kept on smiling. The sort of money Geoffrey's family had to spend . . .

One was cleverer. For the last stop of his tour, he pulled up at something completely different. Two crumbling gate-pillars in a wall of mellow Georgian brick. With stone balls on top. Well, one ball anyway; the other lay beside the weedy drive.

A long narrow house of two storeys. Some bits tagged on afterwards. All covered with horrible damp 1930s pebble-dash, but with thick-sashed Georgian windows.

And as Geoffrey pointed out nastily, an estate of cheap *two*-bedroom semis, steadily creeping up the hill to its garden wall.

But the door was six-panelled, and the passage behind paved with rough stone flags. So was the kitchen, which had a long low mullioned window looking out on a beautiful ruined garden.

'End of the seventeenth century,' said the house-agent coaxingly, 'or beginning of the eighteenth. Pity about the *area*, of course,' he waved at the two-bedroom semis, 'but cheap accordingly. And an acre of paddock for the children's ponies.'

'No thanks,' said Geoffrey, shuddering.

It was enough to send her floating down the long narrow passage. How well her grandfather clock would look here! And late seventeenth century! Henry Marlborough *must* have visited, walked through these rooms. She glanced everywhere, expecting a sign. Initials carved in a newel-post; or engraved on the old glass of the windows with his diamond ring. She would *never* get nearer to him than this. Henry Marlborough, are you there?

She walked back to the waiting men.

'I want it,' she said. 'After a survey and if the price is right.' She sounded oddly like her father; it was enough to demolish Geoffrey.

The first architect Geoffrey hired to civilise what he called 'the hovel' lasted precisely one tour of inspection. He proposed demolishing the tall chimneys as unsafe, covering the stone flags with lino-tiles, and replacing the sash windows with double-glazed fakes.

She told him to go and castrate somebody else's house, and fled to Miles in a rage.

'Young Hughie Megson's the one you want,' said Miles, lighting another fag with yellow-stained fingers, and letting it droop from the corner of his mouth like the real newspaper-man she loved.

'What's so marvellous about young Hughie Megson?'

'He's just finished Babbington Hall for the National Trust . . . '

'He *might* do,' she said.

He did do. Thin, bespectacled, frizzy-haired Hughie Megson was real as well. Said he had an ancestress, Lady Caroline Megson, who had been a minor mistress of Charles II. She liked the modesty of that 'minor' bit.

Together, they had great moments. Discovering lost doors under twenty layers of wallpaper. Exposing oak beams above Victorian ceilings. There was even a tiny lost staircase inside a walled-up cupboard. And a well, set in the stone flags of the kitchen. They bought a Victorian cast-iron pump, that pumped water straight into the stone trough of a sink; a sink Hughie Megson was sure *must* be eighteenth century. They kept the Victorian kitchen range. When she came to see how the men were getting on, she scrounged scrap wood from them and lit a fire in the grate, and warmed her hands and felt at home.

Every so often, Geoffrey put in an appearance and bleated about kitchen units and central heating. Hughie put in some extra-discreet central heating to keep him quiet.

Meanwhile, she paid the price. Slept with Geoffrey as often as required. Lay back and thought about Henry Marlborough.

When she finally got herself pregnant, it was a relief to them both. Honour satisfied, duty accomplished, they took to separate bedrooms.

The morning her pregnancy was confirmed, she drove down to the house. They were carefully stripping off the pebble-dash, displaying beautifully coursed sandstone that had not seen the light of day for fifty years.

'Got something to show you,' said Hughie.

In the stonework above the door, a date had been laid bare.

1689.

Henry Marlborough would have been fifty-seven. A middle-aged man, with his five children off his hands . . . it *must* be his new house.

There were dim crumbling shadows in the stone, each side of the date. She stared at them, trembling. Could that be an 'H'? An 'M'?

'What do you make of it?' she asked Hughie, breathless.

'Could be an "M",' he said. 'The house is called Marler's End by the locals. "M" for "Marler". But the rest is gone. They set the lintel the wrong way, and it's crumbled with the weather.'

She just *knew*. Marler. A corruption over the years of 'Marlborough'. Her eyes filled with tears. Somehow, he had brought her home. Somehow, she was the new wife he had waited for, for three centuries. She scanned the vague blurred shadows on the other side of the date. Was that a 'Z'?

'The other side could be anything,' said Hughie brutally. 'Pity about the weathering.'

They quarrelled endlessly about the furnishings. Everything Geoffrey suggested drove her mad. In the end, because they had to start living in the house, they divided it between them. He filled his study with glass and steel hi-tech, and the lounge and dining room with crushed velvet and repro Regency. He had his fitted kitchen; in the old laundry.

She kept her unfitted kitchen. She cooked in his and sat in hers, baking stoneground wholemeal bread with live yeast, the way Henry Marlborough would have liked it. As the incense of it rose soothingly to her nostrils, she rocked and apologised out loud to the oil painting for Geoffrey's insults to his house.

It was her father, of all people, who put the idea of writing a novel into her mind. He called to congratulate her yet again on her pregnancy, and to say he was putting the boy's name down for Eton. She refrained from asking him what he would do if it was a girl. Her desire to fight him frightened her now.

'How d'you fill your days in?' he asked. 'Still scribbling? One of them Mills and Bomb novels, is it?' He laughed uproariously at his own joke.

But when he'd gone, the thought stayed with her. Why shouldn't she write a novel? She still had seven months of pregnancy and peace, before the kid's bawling would turn her brain into a pulp.

Even with a pulped brain, she might still scribble the odd article. But a novel would be out of the question for *years*.

Now or never.

But what about?

She rocked gently in her chair, eyes shut, mind searching timidly outwards.

Into the silence, broken only by the ticking of the grandfather clock, a thought came drifting.

Henry Marlborough had been a boy in the Civil War.

Both armies had passed through Smilesby, on their way to the Battle of Marston Moor. Young Henry, aged fourteen, might have stood at his father's gate, staring open-mouthed as first Prince Rupert and then Cromwell rode through at the head of their men. Young Henry, riding to warn Prince Rupert, caught and brought before the brutal Cromwell? (Cromwell immediately assumed her father's face.)

She got up to do the washing-up. But as she started, a kind of hurricane hit her. Plot, characters, dialogue, boiled up and twisted together in her brain. Like jam boiling too fast. Like a volcano erupting.

When she came out of it finally, the washing-up was still not done, and the water had gone stone-cold. She pulled her hands out of it and looked at them. They were white and shrivelled and wrinkled like an old woman's hands. Not her hands at all.

She shivered, though the weather was quite warm. She felt she had been possessed. She had never felt like that in her life before.

She wrote and wrote, and it was no good. She'd thought she knew everything about old Smilesby, but she knew *nothing*. She didn't even know what kind of trousers Henry Marlborough might have worn, or what he ate for breakfast.

She wrote dialogue full of 'forsooths' and 'prythees' then tore it up screaming with rage. She wrote without 'forsooths' and it sounded like two housewives chatting over the garden fence.

She drove thirty miles to a Sealed Knot battle, in

the guise of a reporter for the *Smilesby Advertiser*. The sweating Roundheads and Cavaliers took time off to chat her up (even pregnant she was a very pretty girl) and she came home with her head full of demi-culverins and dragooners and cornets of horse. And how, if you stuck a loaded pistol in your belt, you were liable to end up singing soprano . . . But it all just churned round in her head meaninglessly, like the washing in the washing machine.

She didn't even know if the secret message young Henry was supposed to be carrying would have been written on paper, parchment or vellum.

Again, she tore it all up in a rage, and fled to Miles in tears.

'Oh God,' said Miles. 'I knew it would come to this. Another good female journalist gone to the dogs, for a spot of swashbuckling and bodice-ripping. What about your article for this week's paper?'

She slammed down an article about the Sealed Knot. Maddeningly he picked it up and read it very slowly.

'Not bad,' he said judiciously. 'But not exactly *local*. Not exactly *Smilesby*. I told you bodice-ripping softens the brain.'

Then he grinned and said, 'I owe you one. Go and see Colin Hedge – he knows everything about the history of Smilesby. Just don't ask him anything about the twentieth century, that's all. It's not his period. He gets lost in supermarkets . . . '

'Why haven't you told me about him before?'

'He's a friend of mine. And he's *shy*.'

She kicked him under the desk. But not very hard.

* * *

Colin Hedge was so shy he was an agony to be with. He sat her down in the tiny front room of 9, Laburnum Terrace, and left her just sitting there for twenty minutes. She was beginning to fear he'd fled the house altogether when he came back bearing a tray of tea. The traycloth had crinoline ladies embroidered on it. She looked at him, as he poured the cups with a trembling hand. He was smaller than she was, and painfully thin. His greying hair was cut short-back-and-sides, so his ears stuck out. His grey flannel trousers were baggy at the knees and frayed at the hems.

She looked round the tiny room; at the little tables with barley-sugar legs; at the flying plaster ducks on the wall. All this must be his dead mother's stuff; he lived here alone. She despaired.

'What did you want to know?' he mumbled, offering the sugar-bowl with his head down.

'A man called Henry Marlborough, buried . . . '

'Parish churchyard 1722. Married Martha Barcombe 1660, the year the King returned. Five children. Young Martha 1662, Elizabeth 1663, Caroline 1664, Charles 1666 and James 1668. Martha Barcombe died in childbirth 1669. He was a brewer by trade, and a Royalist in politics.'

He was really looking at her now; she had never seen such pale sharp blue eyes. He was transformed by his enthusiasm; he had all the authority now of a tiny Roman emperor.

'Am I right?' he enquired with a ghost of a grin. How could a person change so, in a moment, she wondered? What must he be like inside? But she only said:

'How do you know he was a Royalist?'

'He could hardly be a Roundhead, with children called Elizabeth, Charles, James and Caroline . . . '

She felt a fool. But she also felt swept off her feet in a most agreeable way. She had found her expert.

She staggered out of the house three hours later, with a full notebook and her head in a whirl. All the technology of seventeenth-century brewing. The fact that young Henry would have eaten only coarse dry bread for breakfast, if his father was poor, or maybe cold roast beef if his father was well off. That his trousers might well have been of fustian. That if the fustian-cutters spoilt a piece of cloth they had to buy it off their master, and got no pay for their day's work, into the bargain . . .

He saw her to the door, telling her one more last thing, then another last thing. About the savage little skirmish in Smilesby, after the battle. How in damp weather, the cobbles of Rye Lane still showed odd stains that were said to be Roundhead blood.

She took his hand in a firm grip and shook it. 'I must go – my husband will be waiting for his meal!'

She watched sadly as the light went out of his eyes, and he suddenly began to blink, then dropped his gaze. It was like . . . killing something beautiful. He was the oddest little man she had ever met, but she felt a great rush of gratitude and affection.

'May I ring you up? If I need more help?'

He nodded silently, and closed his maroon-painted front door. She drove home in such a whirl of the seventeenth century she nearly crashed into a stationary lorry.

Geoffrey had a long wait for his meal that night. It was only tea and toast and boiled eggs, but the toast was burnt, the eggs hard-boiled and the tea as weak as washing-up water.

She crouched over the parish records, in Wretby church vestry.

'Try for his marriage,' said Colin gently. '1660 – but remember part of January comes at the *end* of the year . . . '

She was sure he knew the exact date, the exact page of the records it would be on. But he wanted to give her the pleasure of finding it for herself. That was his way . . . the paper flopped limply under her hand, browning round the edges, but firm and uncrumbling. Paper made from rags, Colin said, rags of linen. Everlasting. The ink had faded to a mid-brown. The seventeenth-century vicar's writing was flowing and elegant. He must have been a Royalist, reinstated. No Puritan could have had such a hand.

And there it was. Henry Marlborough, brewer, bachelor of the parish of St Mary Smilesby. Aged twenty-eight. So young, so hopeful.

Her fingers touched the old writing, and it was as if she had touched Henry Marlborough himself. A shock ran through her, as if her three-month child had stirred. Henry Marlborough must have stood in this very vestry and watched the vicar write. She was warm on the scent, very warm . . .

She lived her pregnancy much more in the seventeenth century than in the twentieth. Wrote and wrote and wrote, tore up and wrote again. Every time she got stuck, she rang Colin. Where would Henry have washed before breakfast? Outside at the pump in his father's yard. What kind of shoes did he wear? Great clumping things with buckles and square toes. Either shoe would fit either foot, so you didn't have to think which one to put on, when you got up in the morning.

They went in her Fiat Panda to Long Marston, and traced out the battle on the fields below, right down to the winding Ouse and the road to Harrogate that was *still* the road to Harrogate even if it was now a broad strip of tarmac full of the flashing of car windscreens. They ate their sandwiches in companionable silence, with the wind hissing through the corn, and the lark ascending, and the calling of distant curlews. To the wind and the corn and the curlews, time was nothing. She thought Henry Marlborough sat with them, in spirit.

'This is where Boy was killed,' said Colin, pointing with a half-eaten sandwich. 'Rupert's big white poodle, who always went with him into battle. The Roundheads said Rupert was a witch, and the dog was his familiar spirit. They shot it.'

She didn't know whether to cry for Boy, or to laugh at the way they could travel through time. But she made a note of Boy, to put him in the book.

Her belly swelled, till she could no longer believe it was part of her. Her ankles swelled. But she drove herself unmercifully. Before the child was born, Henry Marlborough must be re-born. Henry Marlborough must fly out into the world, before the child slammed the door. She might die in childbirth; some women still did. But if the book was out in the world, it wouldn't matter . . .

The doctor became worried; she must rest more. She let a lot of things go; no more dinner-parties for the parents; no more little suppers for Geoffrey and his friends. She pleaded the doctor and her swollen ankles. But the moment Geoffrey left in the mornings, she was at her typewriter.

The baby became due; there was talk of an induced labour. She ceased to tear up chapters, and just wrote and wrote.

That last morning, the present faded totally away, and she was in Prince Rupert's opening charge, with Henry Marlborough. Thigh to thigh she rode with men on either side (it was lucky that her father had once paid for riding lessons, so she knew the feel of a horse under her). She felt the weight and constriction of the iron helmet on her head, with its wire faceguard, because she had borrowed one from a member of the Sealed Knot, and worn it for a whole day. She felt the painful nip of breastplate and backplate, the slow flap of iron greaves on her thighs, as the troop broke into a canter. (Rupert never galloped into a charge.) The rattling of the short carbine, strapped across her breastplate; the fireworks smell from the long pistols ready primed in their saddle-holsters. The smell of sweat from the horse, the foam that was gathering on his black neck, where the rein chafed him. The desperate struggle to keep the horse in line with the others, when he tried to surge forward, or suddenly checked for a rabbit-hole.

There was a terrible urge to sheer away to the left, away from the hawthorn hedge where the Parliamentary dragoons lay in wait; the thin strands of white smoke rising and sudden glints of tiny fire, as the dragoons nervously blew on their matches, to keep them alight.

The surge of terror rising in her throat, as the two lines of cavalry clashed together, and carbines and pistols flashed their erratic pale blooming flames . . .

An hour later, she finished the book, with Henry Marlborough limping home, battle lost, horse lost, weapons thrown away in the terror of pursuit. A country child whose head was filled with visions of agony too great for him to bear. A boy who would never, never fight again.

She wrote 'Ends' and wept for him. Then she was back in her own kitchen, with the grandfather clock ticking in the hall, and the fire burnt low, and she was cold, cold, shivering from head to foot.

Then the first painful twinge in her belly, like a dragging of hot wire.

But she still parcelled up the typescript in a rush, into the envelope long prepared for it, with the address of the publisher she had so carefully researched all those months before.

She drove down to the village post office and sent it off registered.

She never made it home; they sent the ambulance to the post office for her.

She had been home three weeks with the baby when the publisher's letter came. Three weeks of broken nights and bucketfuls of dirty nappies in the cupboard under the sink unit. She was a zombie who, however much she bathed, smelt sickeningly of milk. A cow, a mindless domestic beast who burnt the toast before breakfast and fell asleep over dinner.

She tore the letter open so frantically her thumb gouged the envelope in two, and the two bits fell on the doormat. Phrases swam up at her. 'Thoroughly researched' . . . 'a likeable and convincing hero'. Then nastier bits – 'twice the length of a marketable modern novel' . . . 'over-elaborate descriptions of domestic routine' . . . 'not a great demand for the historical novel at present'. Then, blessedly, 'with severe cutting' and 'we are willing to take a chance' and 'a £1500 advance against royalties, half payable upon completion and half on publication'.

She had made it. She had passed through the waters to the other side.

Upstairs, in his little room, the baby began to cry. She carried the letter up with her. In the process of changing his nappy, it fell out of her housecoat pocket and got badly smeared. She thought it was the two parts of her life coming together, and laughed a little wildly.

When the nappy was finally changed, she hugged the baby to her fiercely. In her zombie way, she loved him. In her mind, he was already called Henry.

Of course, there was a row about the names. Geoffrey wanted him called Timothy George, after each of his grandfathers. That was what all the grandparents wanted too. They thought 'Henry' was old-fashioned, outrageous, ridiculous. Nobody in either family had ever been called Henry. It was Victorian, vulgar . . . the waves of disapproval broke over her from both sides. Usually at formal gatherings, where she couldn't just pick up the baby and walk away. They could reduce her to tears easily with their bullying, but they couldn't change her mind. It didn't matter what other names the baby was called, as long as one of the names was Henry. She counter-attacked with the only weapon she had; silent white-faced fury.

They even talked the godparents into trying to betray her at the christening. The cowardly godparents gave the vicar the names 'Timothy George' thinking she wouldn't dare make a fuss in public in front of the whole congregation.

She cried out in a loud disagreeable discordant voice, that rang down the church:

'Timothy George *Henry*.'

It was the end of any relationship she still had with Geoffrey. Now they spoke only about things like money and groceries. Every time the grandparents came there was a row, because she insisted on calling the child 'Henry'. Her father made an unforgivable remark about taking her to see a psychiatrist.

But she clung on to the rags of her life. Managed to keep her weekly column going, on what she read in the papers, or with projects she'd dreamed up in freer times, or after long helpful telephone chats with Colin. She worked when she could, cutting and revising the novel. Her new editor was kind, helpful, and above all a woman; she was persuaded eventually to call her 'Marge'. The book acquired a title, *The Sword Upraised*. (She had wanted to call it just *Henry Marlborough* but Marge said that was hopelessly old-fashioned.) Marge now talked about Henry Marlborough as if he was a real person, and that was a great comfort. Colin helped over the phone, as always. He was much more confident over the phone; even made little jokes. He had found out for her the old site of Marlborough's brewery. He took her to see it. Sadly, it had vanished totally under a small factory making double-glazing. But it *had* been on the main road to Marston Moor. Henry Marlborough *could've* stood at his father's gate and watched Rupert ride by at the head of his men.

The last evening came with Geoffrey. The worst row ever. About the baby's name, the grandparental wrath, her coldness towards him, the lack of sex, and much more important, the lack of entertaining, so he couldn't ask his friends home any more. He gave her an ultimatum. Either he would have things his way in future or he was packing his bags and leaving . . .

'Yes,' she said. 'You'd better go. There's some clean shirts in the airing cupboard. Don't forget them when you pack.'

She felt just weary and relieved. The end of a long, long lie. She had enough to do, without looking after him. Marge was asking about the possibility of a second book about Henry Marlborough 'in case the first goes down all right'. She'd sounded quite optimistic.

It was a nasty moment when the front door banged shut behind Geoffrey. But she just sat and rocked, little Henry on her lap, asleep after his feed. The smell of the afternoon's bread-baking still lingered in the air. The house creaked, in a friendly way. There was the smell, mingling with the smell of baking, of dust and old time. Her grandfather clock ticked, soothingly. She knew Henry Marlborough was near. Just Henry and her and little Henry now . . . she slept, and dreamt that the portrait of the middle-aged man in the floppy white shirt began to breathe gently.

* * *

Her success, when it came, was pure fluke. As Marge said, the book shouldn't have got more than a few kind words in *History Today*. But there was a famous left-wing TV producer who wanted to make a protest about the brutality of war; a kind of counterblast to *By the Sword Divided* which had just had a great success. And there was a rising young pop-star, with a tragic, ravaged face, who wanted to have a go at being an actor. And lots of bands of young men, now, only too willing to dress up in Civil War armour and batter each other to bits for nothing, let alone the technicians' wages that ITV paid them . . .

She sold the TV rights for forty thousand. And the paperback, brought out to coincide with the series, would sell two hundred thousand copies.

But to Zillah, none of it was a fluke. It was Henry Marlborough, taking care of her, as he always did . . . She had a nanny now, an unmarried mum called Susan, quite happy to look after young Henry for board and lodging and a few quid in notes that the social security never heard about. Susan was so old-fashioned she called Zillah 'ma'am'. They had cosy evenings in front of the old kitchen range, making bread and discussing Susan's boy-friends. Zillah tried not to be too cynical about marriage; she didn't feel she was any kind of expert . . .

When the second Henry Marlborough book, the one that took him up to his marriage, was done and sent off to Marge, she held a little thank-you party for Miles and the boys from the paper. Colin had come too, but had gone all maddeningly humble, and spent the evening handing round things to eat, and washing up.

Young Henry was the centre of her life; him and the

writing. And there was Henry Marlborough's house to look after. She had used her TV money to buy up Geoffrey's half, and now felt every inch the householder, inspecting her slates after every high wind.

She never missed Geoffrey; there was simply too much to do. And in the evenings, when she was totally knackered, she just sat and rocked and dozed in her chair, and felt the gentle patient spirit of Henry Marlborough creak and sigh his way around her, enclosing her with his approval.

All for Henry. She was exhausted and fulfilled.

Until the sunny evening she went for a drive in her new Fiat Uno. And, over towards Wretby, came upon a pair of gateposts with urns on top she knew well. She had often wondered nosily about them. But they had always looked so bleak and unwelcoming; the gates rusted and shut, and a mass of sullen green rhododendrons encroaching on a weedy drive.

Now, all was transformed; the gates new-painted, the bushes cut back, Victorian streetlamps with shining copper tops installed, and a smart sign saying

THE WRETBY MANOR HOTEL.
FRENCH CUISINE.

She didn't even try to resist temptation; just drove straight in. If it matched the gateposts, Wretby Manor must be quite a stately home.

And it was. Stone quoins, high-pitched roof with a cupola on top. William-and-Mary style, about 1695, she judged. Her period. Henry Marlborough might have visited. She settled in the nearly empty bar, ordered a dry martini, and took out her notebook . . .

But as she squinted around, disapproving of the repro armchairs, a sign caught her eye. It was in gilded Gothic lettering, and almost unreadable, but it seemed to say

TO THE MARLBOROUGH BAR

She followed the signs. And then came upon the mural: a slick, cheap and nasty mural. Of a fat laughing old man with a white beard, absurdly dressed like 'The Laughing Cavalier' but looking more like Falstaff. Especially with the huge spilling tankard in his hand, and the half-naked doxies, almost coming out of their dresses, who sat at his feet or leant over his chair, tickling him archly under the chin, like a bunch of Rank starlets.

'Who is this supposed to be?' she positively hissed at a passing waiter. The waiter took one look at her face, said he hadn't a clue, and fetched the manager. The manager, idle as yet, and proud of his new hotel, was full of information.

'That's Sir Henry Marlborough, who built this house, madam, in the seventeenth century. 1698. A wealthy brewer from Smilesby. Made his pile buying up cheap land that the King had confiscated from the Puritans. A right shark he seems to have been. And a right one for the ladies in his old age. Merrie England, and all that!' The manager sniggered suggestively, and Zillah didn't know whether to throw her drink at him, or at the stupid, *stupid* mural. So in the end she just put it down carefully on a beaten-copper table, drove home like a madwoman, and rang Colin, livid at such an outrage.

'No, it's all true,' said Colin miserably, after a long silence. 'I've known for a bit . . . '

'Why on earth didn't you *tell* me?'

Another long silence, then Colin said desperately:

'Didn't want to upset you. You were so keen to make him a *hero*. And you were so sure you were living in his house . . . '

'But . . . Marler's End . . . Marlborough's End!' She felt the earth crumbling beneath her feet.

'There was a Marler. A Thomas Marler. A rabid Puritan, fined five shillings at Smilesby Court Left in 1661, for making treasonable remarks about the new King. One thing you can be quite sure of. Henry Marlborough was never in your house. The pair of them must have been like chalk and cheese and nasty with it.'

'And was Henry a . . . lecher?'

'Famous for it, throughout the county. At the height of his wealth, he had this huge alabaster memorial effigy made for himself, for the parish church. Him lying there, in full armour mind you, with his mistresses kneeling around him in prayer. Aubrey records a joke epitaph:

> 'Here lies the good old knight Sir Harry
> Who loved well, but would not marry.
> While he was live, and had his feeling
> They did lie, and he was kneeling.
> Now he is dead, and cannot feel
> He doth lie, and they do kneel.'

'Is it still there?' She grasped at straws.

'No, the vicar wouldn't give it house-room. It was

sold off cheap and ground up as a cure for croup in sheep. He lost everything in the end, with his drinking and his wenching . . . big house, the lot . . . '

'He hath builded his house on sand,' she said bitterly.

'Perhaps he really set out to find a new wife, in the beginning. Perhaps he found the women too willing . . . '

'But . . . he must have done something brave, to get knighted.'

'You could buy a knighthood in those days – easy money for the Crown. Sometimes rich men were *forced* to buy knighthoods, if the King was hard up.'

She rang off in despair She had had more historical truth than she could bear.

It was late. The children and Susan long in bed. She sat and rocked, waiting for her friendly ghost to steal gently over her, with a creak and a sigh. But *who*? *Never* that wretched lecherous old bankrupt! *Never* the Puritan Marler! He was gentle, quite, patient, approving . . . he would *still* look after her.

But there was nothing. The creaks remained creaks; the sighs only the sound of the wind. A hundred times she hoped, and a hundred times she was disappointed.

She slowly began to doubt the house was haunted after all. And grew more and more terrified. Nothing, living or dead, desired her. Nothing would ever come again.

She realised for the first time that *nothing* was more terrifying than any ghost.

Unable to bear the silence any more, she rang Colin again.

'Colin? I . . . thought this house was haunted. Well, it's not.'

'I know.' Colin sounded like a ghost himself, very far away, on the dark side of the moon.

'But, Colin . . . something made me do those things . . . buy this house . . . write the books. *Somebody* helped me . . . '

'Well . . . Miles and the lads . . . ' How typical, she thought, that he should not mention himself.

'Oh, I know *that*. And I'm grateful. But there was somebody else, when I needed him.'

'Maybe it was just . . . part of yourself?'

'Colin, I'm *nothing*.'

'Nothings don't write books. Nothings don't get famous.'

He meant it to be encouraging; but it sounded awful. Nothings *did* write books and get famous, and buy houses and get rid of husbands and drive away fathers and mothers. Nothings could climb so high they became frightened to move for fear of falling.

'Thanks, Colin,' she said, dreary with inner terror. 'Good night.' Obediently, he rang off. She listened to the click and the dialling tone.

She sat and rocked again, and the rocking mocked her. The whole world mocked her, because it was empty. Nothing was going to happen to her, for the rest of her life. Nothing, over and over again, till the day she died.

She sat, going slowly mad, till midnight. Please come, she said in her mind, something, *anything*. She must have fallen asleep from the sheer stress of nothing.

She was awakened by the hollow sound of the front

door-knocker. The grandfather clock said 1 a.m. Who could possibly be knocking on her door at 1 a.m.? Nothing in this world . . .

And yet a quaint little thought came curling through the dreariness of madness. Something outside that door wanted her and anything was better than nothing. Anything it did to her was better than this endless pointlessness . . .

She got up, smoothed her dress, gave herself a smile in the mirror as she passed it, that was the smile of a madwoman.

I will give myself to whatever is knocking on the door. He can do what he likes with me. It was odd that, even then, she thought it might be a *he*.

She hesitated once, with her hand on the key. There was silence outside now; whatever it was had not knocked again.

Then she opened the door.

'Hello,' said Colin, blinking. 'Sorry if I got you up, but I was worried about you.'

'Come in,' she said.